S0-BRP-470

SHARING
SUSAN

SHARING SUSAN

a novel by

Eve Bunting

A TRUMPET CLUB SPECIAL EDITION

Published by The Trumpet Club
666 Fifth Avenue, New York, New York 10103

ISBN 0-440-84962-4

This edition published by arrangement with HarperCollins
Children's Books, a division of HarperCollins Publishers

Printed in the United States of America
Typography by Joyce Hopkins
January 1993

1   3   5   7   9   10   8   6   4   2
OPM

To Chris and Richard,
Debbie and Sloan

Chapter 1

I knew bad things were happening at home. I just didn't know what they were.

My friend Clemmie and I called it the Big Worry. To help me out, Clemmie kept planning neat things we could do together so I'd forget to worry for a while. Today she was hurrying me home from school because her big sister, Sophia, had just taught her how we could find out the initials of our future husbands.

"Hurry up, Susan," Clemmie urged. "Just think! You might get A.L. Wouldn't that cheer you up, huh? He's definitely the cutest boy in sixth grade. Wouldn't it cheer you up to get him for your future husband?"

"I guess." I didn't want to sound ungrateful. But truthfully, I couldn't think of anything that would cheer me up right now.

"Last night Mom and Dad were talking in the living room," I told Clemmie, walking fast to keep up. We had just turned the corner into our street, and Douglas, the big dog who lives in the house across from us, came lolloping over to greet us. I gave him my hand to slobber.

"The minute my parents saw me," I went on, "they stopped talking and smiled those awful fake smiles."

"Maybe you got it all wrong. Maybe they're just planning a big surprise," Clemmie suggested. "A happy surprise."

"Whatever it is, it's not happy. I told you, I've heard Mom crying three times in the bathroom. Three times. And once in the kitchen. I saw her. She was making coffee, and these big tears were running down her face." I tried not to let my voice shake, but it did and I turned my head away.

Clemmie slowed. "How about if we split a banana? I saved one from lunch." She waggled out of her backpack straps, found the banana, peeled it, gave me half. "I find bananas very calming," she said, dropping the peel back among her books.

I nodded, took a bite and broke off a piece for Douglas Dog. The three of us started walking again.

"Do you want to talk about our future husbands or—the Big Worry?" Clemmie asked. "It's your choice."

Clemmie is great like that. I'm really lucky to have her for a best friend, especially at a time like this.

"Let's go through the worry possibilities one more time," I said. "The first is that my parents could be getting a divorce."

"Can't be," Clemmie said quickly. "They're too friendly. And didn't they go to San Francisco last week for two passionate days alone together?"

"*You* called them passionate days. They didn't. They just said it was a business trip. And that's weird, too. Second possibility, they've lost their jobs."

We decided this didn't seem likely either since they both work up at the University—U.C. Santa Cruz. Not too many librarians, which Mom is, or professors of art, which Dad is, get fired from there.

"Maybe they've been swindled out of all their money," I said. But I didn't believe that, either. I don't think we *have* much money. Clemmie's father might interest a swindler because he's rich and owns a big artichoke-packing plant in Watsonville. But not us. The fourth possibility I didn't even want to mention again, though we had already—that one of my parents was incurably ill, or that Grandma or Grandpa Moretti, or Grandpa Lucas, was. But they all seemed so healthy. Besides, Grandma and Grandpa Moretti called every weekend from Italy, where they and Aunt Lissa lived. I'd talked to them myself last Sunday. It's

3

harder to know about Grandpa Lucas. He's always on the go since Grandma died. His big motor home has so many place stickers on the back, it looks like a moving billboard. But we'd had a card from him this week. He was passing through Vancouver, Canada. No reason to think he wasn't OK.

Clemmie had thought of number five. "Maybe your mom is having a new baby."

"But my mom would *like* a baby," I said. "And she'd tell me."

"I know. Your parents tell you everything," Clemmie said.

I nodded. "That's what makes this so scary. It must be something humongous."

We walked in silence till we got to Clemmie's house.

She and I live next door to each other, but our house is small and old. Nice, though. Clemmie's is big and fancy. That's the way most streets are in Santa Cruz, a real hodge-podge.

"No city planning worth talking about," Dad says with satisfaction. "Man! Are we ever lucky!"

Clemmie pointed across the street to Douglas Dog's house.

"Go home now. Good doggie!"

Douglas gave a pleading whine and lay down with his nose on his paws.

"No. You're not allowed to come in. I'm sorry,"

4

Clemmie said. Douglas can't come in our house, either. My mom is allergic to just about every animal that ever lived and any plant that ever bloomed. Besides, both our parents think he has fleas.

Clemmie opened the front door and I went in behind her. Usually I wait in her house till I hear Mom and Dad arrive home. It works out great.

As soon as we were inside, we heard the sounds of the TV from the family room and the shouts of Clemmie's little brothers, the two noisiest kids on the block.

"We're home, Mom," Clemmie called, and her mom called back, "Hi, girls."

"We're going to get something to eat and go up to my room," Clemmie yelled. "Mom and Sophia are probably making more lists in there," she whispered to me. "I swear, ever since Sophia got engaged that's all they do, make lists, lists, lists."

We helped ourselves to two cartons of apple juice and a box of crackers and headed upstairs.

As soon as we got in her room, we dropped our backpacks, our school blazers and our clumpy black-and-white shoes and settled on the floor with our backs to the bed.

"Are you sure this initial thing works?" I asked.

Clemmie poked a hole in her juice carton with her straw. "Of course it works. The first letter of the word

5

you pick is the initial of his first name. The last letter is the initial of his last name. Simple! Sophia got B.T. twice. Boomer Thomson. And now she's engaged to him."

Clemmie jumped up, got the book of Emily Dickinson poetry from her dresser and laid it on the bed, smoothing the pale-blue comforter so it didn't puff up around the book.

"But shouldn't it have been W.T.?" I asked. "Isn't Boomer's real name William?"

"You can't expect Emily Dickinson to know *that*," Clemmie said. "She's *dead* anyway. Everybody calls him Boomer.

"Now," she ordered, "scoot around and open the book. Wipe your hands first."

I wiped them on my plaid skirt. Last year our school adopted uniforms for all students because they said we were getting too trendy in our designer jeans, even the little third and fourth graders. We sure aren't trendy now. I opened the book somewhere about the middle.

"Close your eyes," Clemmie said. "Run your finger along a line and say the Emily thing."

"Why do I have to go first?" I asked.

"Because you're my guest, and because, well . . . this is going to help you forget . . . you know."

I nodded, although the worry never really goes

6

away. It backs off and sits, like a jungle tiger waiting to pounce.

"Say the Emily thing or it won't work," Clemmie warned.

I closed my eyes, took a deep breath and said:

> "Emily, Emily let me see
> Who my husband's going to be.
> Carrots, broccoli, spinach, peas—
> Give me his initials, please."

"Let your finger stop, now, fast." Clemmie was out of breath.

I stopped.

Clemmie jiggled my elbow and gave my hand a little shove.

"Susan!" she screamed. "You *got* A.L. Andy Luckinbill. You *lucky*! I can't believe it. You stopped on 'all.'"

"Wait. Are you sure? I thought you jiggled . . . ?"

"No. No. You got him. Doesn't that make you feel better?"

I wanted to tell her it did, and certainly sometime it would be nice to marry Andy Luckinbill. Even in the middle of the Big Worry I felt a ping of excitement. But the ping wasn't as strong as it should have been.

"Your turn, Clem," I said.

Clemmie said the Emily Dickinson thing and stopped at "leaving."

"L.G.? L.G.?" She tapped her thumbnail against her teeth. "We don't know any L.G.s."

"I should have jiggled you," I said apologetically. "I'm not concentrating."

"Don't worry. He's probably someone romantic and passionate who I'm going to meet later."

We sat again with our backs to the bed, the open book behind us.

"It's funny you got the word 'leaving'," I said. "What if that's the answer to the Big Worry? What if we have to move to another city away from Santa Cruz."

"You're serious!" Clemmie said. "Don't even think that. That's horrible."

"Face it, Clemmie, everything we come up with is horrible."

I looked across at the drawing Dad had made of Clemmie and me. I'd framed it in blue construction paper to match her room and had given it to her for Christmas last year. Now it hung above her dresser. There we were, Clemmie short and round with her wispy hair coming out of her ponytail, me tall and standing kind of droopy, the way I'm not supposed to stand. My overgrown spike haircut made me look a bit like the Statue of Liberty. Dad is magical at drawing. Clemmie and I looked real enough to step out of the

8

blue frame and be twins of ourselves. Across the top Dad had printed SUSAN AND CLEMENTINE, THE BEST OF FRIENDS.

My eyes started to sting. I remembered him doing the drawing in just a few quick strokes, the way he'd hugged me after and said: "My very own pinup girl." I remembered the way we'd smiled at each other. There'd been no Big Worry in sight then.

I stood up, fumbling for my shoes. "I think I'll go home, Clem," I said.

"But . . ." Clemmie stopped. "It's only a quarter to five. Your parents aren't home yet. Are you sure you want to be by yourself? The tiger might come."

I'd told her about the tiger and the way he liked to jump out at me when everything was quiet and when I was alone.

Somehow one of my shoes had gotten all the way underneath the bed and Clemmie wriggled in to get it for me.

"You know what I'd do?" she said when she'd wriggled back out. "I'd ask them again."

"They'd probably say the same thing. 'Yes, something is wrong. But we're hoping it won't come to anything, and we'd rather not bring you into it if we don't have to.'"

Mom had held me tight. "Trust us, Susan. Can you

9

do that? Just for a little while."

"But this time, if I were you, I'd cry when I asked," Clemmie said. "I'd really throw a fit. Tell them no matter how bad it is you'd rather know. Say, 'I can't stand it anymore!'"

I got my blazer and stuffed my shoes into my backpack. "I *can't* stand it anymore," I said. "I think I will ask again."

"Call me. OK?"

We trailed down the stairs together.

"'Bye."

"Keep thinking about A.L.," Clemmie called after me.

"I'll try," I said.

I got the key from the hanging pot of impatiens on our porch and let myself in, fumbling a little because the phone was ringing and that makes me crazy. I dropped everything and slid across the floor to get it.

"Hello?"

"Hello?" It was a man's voice. "Are your parents there?"

I knew not to answer that . . . not when I was alone and didn't recognize the caller. "Who is it please?" I asked instead.

There was a pause. "I guess I'm too early. They're probably not home yet." Another pause. "Is this Susan?" Strange how his voice changed, softened when he said my name.

I didn't say yes or no because that isn't too smart a thing to do either, when you're by yourself.

"Well, this is David DiGrasso." Now he was all businesslike again. "Would you please ask your dad to call me as soon as he gets in. I'll be at the office for another hour. He knows my number."

"I'll tell him," I said.

"Thank you." There was only buzzing on the line now. I hung up and wrote "David DiGrasso" on the little memo pad and stood looking down at it. Who was he? What office was he calling from? How come he knew me?

And then there was that strange, strange feeling I'd had when he said my name. As if he knew something. As if he was sorry for me.

Chapter 2

David DiGrasso had said Dad had his number. I flipped through the small alphabetized phone book on the kitchen counter, and there it was—DiGrasso, David. What would happen if I called and said . . . ? Before I could think about it too much and get nervous, I dialed.

A woman's brisk voice said: "Jepson, Jepson, DiGrasso and Smith."

Very quietly I hung up, muttering the names over and over as I got out the big phone directory.

The listing was there all right. Attorneys at Law. Smith was spelled Smythe.

I began listing possibilities, the way Clemmie does. Why do people go to see attorneys? They make wills.

They get help because they've done something wrong. They need advice. I paced around our living room with its bare white walls hung with Dad's paintings, like some of the modern art galleries we've visited. Yes, parents who go to see a lawyer could definitely be planning a divorce.

I imagined Dad saying: "We have one daughter, Susan. We want you to work things out, Mr. DiGrasso." Would I stay with Mom or Dad? Would they divide me, so much time here, so much time there? And where was there? Not much wonder David DiGrasso had sounded sorry for me.

Clemmie had wanted me to think about A.L. How could I now? How could I think of anything but this?

A car stopped out front. I walked slowly to the window. Mom and Dad. They were still in the car, Mom in the passenger seat turned toward Dad.

He was talking while she listened. Then she let her head droop forward and Dad put his hand tenderly on the back of her neck. I've seen him do that a million times. Would he still do it if they were getting a divorce?

I watched Mom and Dad get out and start up the path, neither of them tall, Mom with her shoulder-length straight hair and beautiful pale face, Dad darker skinned, his curly black hair turning gray, his small, neat mustache. Their expressions changed from solemn to vivacious as I opened the door.

"Hi, Susie."

"Hi, love."

"Hi. Jepson, Jepson, DiGrasso and Smythe called."

"David called?" Dad asked.

Did I imagine that Mom's face got even paler?

"He said he's still at the office and he'd like you to phone him," I said.

Dad smiled brightly at me. "OK. How about if you fix some cheese and crackers and iced tea to hold us till dinner?"

Mom nodded. "Good idea, Susan."

They were looking at me as if this was some wonderful new plan they'd suddenly thought up, as if we didn't follow the same routine every night.

"Sure." I padded around the counter and into the kitchen.

We have only one phone and it's right there, right on that counter, but there's a long cord so it can be carried all the way through into the living room.

Dad made the call, standing with his back to me, speaking softly as he stared out the front window. Mom sat on the edge of the couch, listening.

The waxed cracker paper rustled. The ice clinked in the glass. It was hard to hear. A word or phrase came to me now and then.

"Did they seem . . . ?"

"We don't want to have to go through . . ."

And then, in a sudden lull, I heard two or three complete sentences spoken in a dull, resigned voice that didn't sound like my dad at all.

"Yes. We'll take her in tomorrow. I guess there's no point in putting it off any longer."

I was the "her" who was going to be taken somewhere tomorrow. I knew that for sure. The fear came again. Where were we going? What for?

"Good-bye, David," Dad said. "I'll let you know."

Clemmie had advised me to throw a fit, to cry so I could find out what was happening. But I didn't need to pretend. I was crying anyway, my chest so tight I thought it would explode if I didn't.

Dad quickly hung up the phone and then he was beside me, his arms around me. Mom was there, too.

"You're getting a divorce," I said. "It's true, isn't it?" My voice was muffled against his shoulder.

"No sweetie, no." Mom stroked my hair, and in the long silence I sensed some sort of eye communication between them.

Then Dad said: "But there is something we have to tell you, Susan. We hoped it would go away. We'd hoped with David's help we could make it go away. But we can't."

They were easing me gently between them out of the kitchen and toward the couch. We sat down. I

15

looked from one of them to the other. "What? Tell me."

I remember that the last sunlight was coming through the window filling the cool pale room with its golden glow. I remember the diamond sparkle of the ice in the glasses, the mist on the amber pitcher of tea on the kitchen counter. Mom leaned forward and took both my hands in hers.

"You know how much your dad and I love you, have always loved you. You are our darling child. But we just learned, just found out a few weeks ago . . ." her voice faltered.

"Susan," Dad said, "you remember that you were born in Northridge? Your mom and I were still in college and . . ."

"Doctor's Hospital," I said. "December twenty-third. Mom could hear carolers outside in the corridor. They were singing 'Silent Night.'"

"Yes." Mom let go of my hands then and put her fingers over her eyes as if the brightness of the room hurt her.

"Susan," Dad said. "Honey. There were five babies born that December twenty-third. Two were girls, three were boys." He paused. "There's no easy way to tell you this. I don't know how to. The hospital suspects now that they gave us the wrong little girl."

Chapter 3

I couldn't understand what Dad had said. It didn't make sense.

"The wrong little girl?" I repeated, my voice coming from far, far away. "You mean me? I'm the wrong little girl?"

"No. Never. You're our little girl, Dad's and mine." My mother had taken my hands again, squeezing them too tightly, hurting me, jiggling them up and down as though we were doing some strange exercise.

"But . . . but . . . I don't get it."

"They think a nurse may have made a mistake. They think there was a mix-up at the hospital. The parents of the other little girl discovered it." I'd never heard anything as scary as Dad's voice, as if it was a true fact.

"How could there be a mix-up? That couldn't hap-

pen. That's silly. They're just saying it now because . . .
Anyway, how could they know? It's so long ago.
Twelve years. Mom? It's not true. Tell me. Tell Dad."

But Mom was crying soundlessly, her mouth
twisted, her face ugly. I'd never seen her look like this.

"It's . . . Oh sweetie!" Dad gathered me onto his lap
the way he used to do when I was little. It doesn't work
so well now because I'm so long and dangly, but I made
myself small and curled against him, sniffing him, the
linseed oil and turpentine smell, the Dad smell.

"Do you believe them?" I whispered. "That I'm
somebody else's and not yours?"

"No," Mom said, loud as loud.

"Susie," Dad said. "We don't want to believe them.
In the beginning we wouldn't. But we have to con-
sider it a possibility. I've had blood tests. So has your
mom. So have the Stobbels. And . . . and Marlene."

"The Stobbels?"

"That's their name, honey. Marlene, well . . .
Marlene was the name they gave their little girl. The
blood tests showed they couldn't be Marlene's parents. Then, when the hospital checked the births for
that night . . ." He stroked my hair. "Their lawyers
contacted us. They asked your mom and me to get
tested, too."

"But why did you? Why didn't you say no . . . no . . ."

"Baby, there are all kinds of lawyers and legalities involved. Our lawyer, theirs, the hospital's. The thing is Susie, if we don't go, don't take you for a blood test, they'll get a court order."

Dad rubbed the place between my shoulders that ached so badly. He always knew where I hurt and how to help.

"I don't understand how the tests can be so sure." Panic made me tremble, my knees, my arms, my voice.

"It's like paint," Dad said. "You know how if you mix blue and yellow you get green? And if you don't get green something had to be wrong with the colors to begin with? It's like that. There's something called the Rh factor. And there's a chromosomal test. Heaven knows how they work. But they can say who can or cannot be the parents of a child. The tests we took showed we could be Marlene's mother and father—the Stobbels couldn't."

I curled back against him, even smaller. When I was little I used to suck my thumb, but I was too big for that now.

"Are you saying I'm definitely theirs and not yours?" I asked. "Are you? Will you take her and give me to them?"

Mom made a small moaning sound.

"Susan, we're going to do everything in the world to prove that you are our daughter. It's going to be tough. These tests will be hard to beat. If only we'd never found out! But we did find out, and once that happens, nothing can ever be the same. We're going to fight, though, Susan. Fight! Fight! Fight!"

I slid off his lap. "Will we win?"

"I can't promise you that, Susan. I wish I could."

Outside on the street I could hear Clemmie's little brothers playing catch, shouting to each other. I walked to the window. Across from us Mrs. Cram's yard was its usual muddled mess. Old furniture sat abandoned on the grass, the rusted refrigerator, the claw-footed bathtub that Douglas Dog usually sleeps in. "Only in Santa Cruz," Dad had said with a smile, and he'd done a painting of the yard, bathtub and all.

"Where do they live? The Stobbels?" I asked.

"They live in Laguna Niguel. It's outside of Los Angeles," Dad said.

"We've met them," Mom added. She blew her nose, blew it again. "They're . . . very nice. They flew up and met us in San Francisco."

I suddenly didn't want to know anything at all about them. My mother? My father? No! No! "They have a little boy, too," Mom said. "His name is Jeremy. He's four."

I kept my back turned. I didn't care if they had ten little boys.

"If the test I do shows that I'm not me—that I'm her—will I have to go?" Across the street Douglas

20

Dog uncurled himself from the bathtub and ambled over to join in the game of catch. "Will she come here and sleep in my room and have my books and . . . do you want her more than you want me?"

"Sh . . . Sh." Mom laced her arms around me. I felt her stomach warm against my back. "We want you. We want to keep you forever."

"No you don't. You're all set to make me go. You want to change. Please, Mom, don't send me away."

"Susan," Dad said. "Marlene . . . the other girl . . . she died."

"Died?"

I turned, slowly.

"She was riding her bike. She got hit by a van. Her mom said she was going to play tennis and she was riding along a private road that led up to a club they belong to. There was hardly any traffic, and the truck was bringing soft drinks in, and somehow, they said, Marlene wavered out in front of it." I heard the chokiness in his voice and I realized something for the first time. This really *was* Dad's daughter. Mom's too. Marlene. They'd never seen her. They never knew she was theirs, and now she was dead.

"I'm sorry," I whispered.

"She was in a coma for eight weeks," Dad said. "That's when they did the tests. She needed blood, and her parents wanted to give it and . . . and it didn't work and they discovered . . ."

I let myself sit on the edge of the couch. "And so they found out," I said. "And now they want me to come and . . . and replace Marlene. And that's what you want too, because why would you keep some strange girl around who isn't even your daughter?"

Mom put her hands over her eyes. "Susan! That's not fair!"

"No, it isn't. But it's true. And they've got Jeremy. When I go you won't have anybody. You'd think you'd want me to stay, but oh no! I've been here forever, but it doesn't matter . . ." I was wailing now. "I hate them. I hate you, too. You're all selfish and cruel."

"Stop it," Dad said. "This isn't going to do any good, Susan. You're the one who's saying the cruel things. Of course they want you . . . if you're their daughter. They're trying desperately to get you. And we're trying just as desperately to keep you. How could you think it could be any other way?"

"I won't do those stupid tests," I whispered. "I won't."

Neither of them spoke. Then Dad's finger came up and gently touched my right eyebrow. My eyebrow is very strange. There's a line down the middle, a small thin white line, like a scar where the hair doesn't grow. Mom used to say it was where a fairy touched me with her wand the night I was born. Dad said it was a dueling scar and he'd pretend to swordfight me.

"Susan," Dad said, "Mr. Stobbel has a line down the middle of his eyebrow, too. We'd been hoping and hoping—your mother looked at him and said, 'Oh . . . I see a fairy touched you with her wand, too,' and he said, 'What?' And of course we both knew he didn't understand. But he will."

Dad turned his head away and Mom gave a little sob. "We're so afraid, Susan."

"I can't stand it if it's true," I said.

"Remember, there's no absolute proof yet." Dad took my hand in both of his. "None. I'm holding on to that."

"None," I repeated. "None." I'd hold on to that, too.

Chapter 4

We didn't go to bed till late, and when I got there I couldn't sleep. I watched the moon slant through my window, watched the star that seemed to hang in the same spot, shining especially for me. I could see my shelf with the shadowy shapes of my stuffed animals, Pooh and Piglet and ugly Ernie from Sesame Street. I could see my playhouse that Dad had made for me. *Susie's House* it said above the door, though tonight the moonlight wasn't bright enough to let me read the letters. If things had been different, it would have been *Marlene's House*. But only maybe. No absolute proof yet. None. The window boxes that Dad and I had painted and filled with cardboard flowers were dark against the lighter walls.

24

"Silver pansies?" Dad had asked me. "Well, why not?"

I got out of bed and squirmed in through the playhouse door. The house had fitted me perfectly when I was three years old. Now I was a giant, my knees curled around the cooking stove with its play pots and pans where I'd made so many broccoli pies. There was the table where I'd had doll tea parties, the little red lantern in the middle. I reached out and switched it on. The batteries were weak. I liked to reach through the window and switch on the lantern and light up my house at nighttime. Its glow turned the inside walls a pale shadowed pink. My pictures hung all around. I never was any good at art, though Dad had made a little easel for me when I was two and we'd painted together side by side in his studio. He'd taught me how to mix colors. And today, when he'd been explaining the blood tests, he'd said, "If you mix blue and yellow you get green." If it turned out to be true, I'd be leaving here. I'd be leaving Mom and Dad and Clemmie and everything. But it wasn't true. There was no absolute truth. It was a bad dream and I'd wake up and still be me. I sat there till the batteries failed and then, cold and stiff, I crept back to bed.

Later when my door opened, I knew it was Mom, and I pretended to be asleep.

She knelt beside my bed, not touching me, not

speaking, just kneeling in absolute stillness. Then she went as quietly as she'd come.

I had to call Clemmie early next morning so she'd know to go on to school without me. "My mom and dad and I have something to do today."

"You're not going to *school*?" she asked. "They're not going to *work*? How come?"

I didn't answer and she lowered her voice to a whisper. "Does it have to do with the Big Worry?"

I turned my back to the kitchen table, where Mom and Dad were drinking coffee, leaving their toast untouched in its basket.

"Yes," I said.

They'd already told me that it would be better not to say anything to anyone about what had happened. The fewer people who knew, the better. "After all, it may turn out to be just a false alarm," Mom said.

Oh Mom, you don't really believe that.

But I knew I'd tell Clemmie. She'd be sorry for me and we'd talk about it and she'd swear she wouldn't tell anyone else and she wouldn't. Clemmie is the best person in the whole world at keeping secrets. I couldn't tell her now, though. Not with Mom and Dad right behind me.

"I'll try to see you after school," I said.

"Meantime, I may go mad," Clemmie said. "Can't

you give me some kind of hint?"

"No," I said.

There was a pause, then she asked, "Is it awful, Susan? Humongously awful?"

I lowered my voice. "The worst," I whispered. "Clem, I have to go."

We got to our doctor's office at nine-thirty. Dr. Cohen's nurse drew the blood from my arm and I looked at it and thought, such a little bit of blood in a glass tube and it could change all our lives.

"Usually it takes a couple of days to get the results from the lab," Dr. Cohen told us. "But the lawyers want them urgently, so we've put a rush on it."

"No hurry," Dad said dryly, and Dr. Cohen laid a hand on his shoulder and said: "We'll have them tomorrow, Jim. I'll be sending you a copy, and of course one to the lawyers. But I'll call you right away and tell you what we find out."

Dad sighed. "Yes. Well, thank you."

Dr. Cohen has the kindest eyes. She smiled down at me. "You can uncross your fingers now, Susan. The test is over."

I uncrossed them. Didn't she know it wasn't getting blood taken that scared me? I'd keep them crossed forever if it would make me be Susan Moretti forever.

We went to Waldo's on the pier for lunch, which

27

was a good idea. I thought Dad and Mom had probably decided it ahead of time. Going home to talk and worry would be hard.

Waldo's was crowded as usual, even though it was early, but we got one of the wooden tables right by the railing. Fishing boats poked their noses through to greet us. Gulls sailed over our heads. Dad ordered big lunches for us, breakfasts really, with Waldo's famous chorizo sausage and French toast. But when the plates came, piled high, none of us seemed to be hungry.

"I won't go to the Stobbels," I said. "That's definite." I tried to sound fierce, but my voice shook.

Dad pushed aside his plate and leaned across the table. "Susan, I want to explain something to you. Your mom and I've had time to think about this. We've read up on other cases . . . this isn't the only time something like this has happened." He sighed. "When David first said we'd need to get the blood tests, your mom and I said, 'Never. No. They'll have to drag us in by force. No way will we go out looking for evidence that Susan isn't ours.' And David said: 'They won't drag you in by force. But the hospital is worried about a lawsuit. They want to get this thing settled. I'm afraid there'll be a court order and you'll have to do it anyway. The more roadblocks you put up, the more publicity there'll be. That would be extra hard on Susan.'" A little smear of butter gleamed in

28

Dad's mustache. I leaned across and wiped it off with my finger.

Dad smiled. "Thanks, sweetie." He took my finger, kissed it lightly, let it go. "David told me we had to watch our step. He said, 'If it turns out that Susan is legally the Stobbel's child, you'll be very dependent on their good will and they on yours. You don't want to be enemies.'"

The way Dad said the words, I could tell he had memorized them. He was saying them they way you'd say words in a play.

A gull tiptoed across the table and took a quick peck of Mom's French toast, took another that pulled it right off the plate. Mom didn't even look at it.

"The thing is," she said, "we may have to be asking the Stobbels for favors . . . for the right to see you . . . to share you. If it turns out you're . . ."

I interrupted. "Why don't you stop *saying* that, Mom. You and Dad have decided I am their daughter. I can tell."

"No. No." Mom took off her dark glasses and rubbed her eyes. "That's not true."

"It is true." I cut a piece of chorizo and put it shakily into my mouth. But I couldn't make my throat swallow and I spat it out into my napkin.

"Susan," Dad said, "we have one thing to be grateful for. The Stobbels seem to be decent people. I think

29

they'll try to be fair . . ."

"Fair? Fair? How can you say that?" Tears bubbled behind my eyes. "They're . . . they're *monsters*."

The gull was coming for my sausage now. I put my hands under the table so I wouldn't scare him away.

"They brought us a picture of Marlene," Dad said.

I watched the gull tear the sausage apart. "Did she . . . did she look like me?" What a stupid question. For a minute I was thinking she was my sister. I tried again. "Did she look like you . . . or Mom?"

"Not really," Dad said. "They let us keep the photograph."

"Would you like to see it?" Mom asked. She'd put her dark glasses back on so I couldn't see her eyes, but I could see me in the dark reflection.

"Yes," I said.

Her purse was on the bench beside her. She took a white envelope out of it. It was stiff, and when she opened the flap I saw that there were two pieces of cardboard to protect the picture that was in between.

Mom didn't look at it herself as she passed it over to me. Marlene had a round face and hair as dark as my dad's. But mine was sort of dark, too. Well, medium dark. That didn't mean anything. She was smiling through almost closed lips, and I saw the edge of her braces. It was a school picture. Nobody smiles in school pictures if they have braces. In her school they must not have had uniforms, or else they let them dress up for photo day, because Marlene was wearing a white blouse with blue flowers on it and a blue cardigan sweater. How could she be dead? She wasn't old enough. The carolers had sung for her that night, too, that night twelve years ago, and now she was dead. I stared and stared at the picture and I didn't know what to say. Wordlessly I passed it back.

"Her mother . . . I mean, Mrs. Stobbel, asked me if I had a picture of you." Mom slid the photograph back in its envelope, and I noticed how gently she held it, how her fingers lingered on it before she carefully put it away. Her Marlene. "I told Mrs. Stobbel I didn't have one with me, and then I remembered the little snapshot in my wallet—you know, the one I like so much."

"In the garden?" I asked. "With the wheelbarrow?"

She nodded, pulled out her wallet and flipped it open to one of the plastic windows. "Here." She set the wallet right side up in front of me.

"Why do you keep this? It's yucko," I said.

There I was, eight years old, barefoot, wearing overalls and an old straw hat. It was when I'd had a boy's haircut, cropped up the back. Mom had tried so hard to stop me having that haircut. "It's cool," I'd said. "But Susan, it's fall. You don't need to be cool." "Oh, Mom. I don't mean that kind of cool. You are so

31

square." Dad liked it right away. He said it showed my good bones. He said there was a lovely line to the back of my neck. In the picture no hair showed at all. I could have been bald.

"You look so happy in the picture," Mom said. "So innocent. Such a little girl."

"I look like a dork," I said, and I was thinking of Marlene in her sweet little blouse and sweater.

"I bet the Stobbels were wishing they could have kept the one they had," I said. My voice was so ugly it even scared the seagull away. "And I bet you'd rather have had Marlene, too."

It was the most awful thought I'd ever had in my life.

Mom moved toward me. "That's not true, Susan. Not true." She held out her hand, but I didn't take it.

I wasn't sure if I believed her or not.

Chapter 5

We got home around three. Mom had one of her bad headaches and said she was going to lie down for a while. I said maybe I'd read some more of my new Anastasia book, and Dad said in that case he'd go out to his studio and do a little work.

In Santa Cruz a couple of years back we had a gigantic earthquake. Practically the whole center of town was turned into rubble, so that instead of neat old brick buildings we had these huge craters. The earthquake was in October, and I remember the Christmas after, we did our shopping in big tents, where the stores used to be, and people were talking about how there'd been a hush in the air before the earthquake hit. How the dogs and cats and hamsters and gerbils had sensed it coming and how they'd broken the eerie silence with their howling. I expect it was only the dogs and cats that howled. For us, the earthquake hit as hard and suddenly as the hammer of God. That's what Mom said it was like, and she was right. We didn't sense anything. One minute our world was fine, and the next it was shattered.

This thing that was happening to us was like the earthquake, and Mom and Dad and I were like the dogs and cats and hamsters and gerbils; we knew it was coming, and we were running around in circles, howling silently. Poor animals. Poor us. Knowing ahead of time was worse, because there was nothing to do but worry and wait for it to hit.

I lay on my bed, looking at the words in the book and making no sense of them.

After a few minutes I tiptoed into the kitchen. The only sounds were the faint murmur of the Mozart that Dad had put on the studio stereo and the sliding as I opened the drawer under the counter and found the package of maps. Back in my room I spread the one of California on my bed.

There was Santa Cruz, snug in the top arch of the bay, there was Los Angeles, and farther down Laguna and Laguna Niguel. So far away. Almost as far as Italy, where Grandma and Grandpa and Aunt Lissa live.

Had anyone told them yet about this? Or Grandpa Lucas? Well, I would. Maybe they could stop it. I got out my best notepaper.

Dear Grandma and Grandpa and Aunt Lissa:The most awful thing has happened! They're saying there has been a mix-up and Mom and Dad aren't my parents and I have to go live with these horrible people that I hate. Can you come get me or send me a plane ticket immediately?

Love, Susan.

I addressed the envelope, stuck on the stamps and began the letter to Grandpa Lucas. I'd send it to his post office box in Kansas City and hope for the best. He'd picked Kansas City for his post box because it's just about the middle of America and he says he's bound to pass through there at least a few times every year.

Grandpa—Please plan to drive to Santa Cruz *as soon as you get this letter* and take me with you. I don't have anyone else I can go to, and Mom and Dad are abandoning me. Don't let anyone stop you. I could meet you outside so no one even knows. We could go

35

somewhere like the North Pole where they'd never find me.

The phone rang just as I finished. The house seemed to tremble around me. Already? The results couldn't be in that fast, could they?

We all three got to the kitchen at the same time. It was Dad who picked up the phone, listened, then said: "Sorry. I don't think we'd be interested."

"Carpet cleaning," he told us, and I let out my breath.

Not one of us said why we'd rushed from three different parts of the house, not one of us said a word.

Mom went slowly back to bed and I decided I'd make her a cup of peppermint tea, hot and steamy, the way she likes it, in her flowered china cup.

When it was ready I carried it carefully to her room, going quietly in case she was asleep already. She wasn't. She lay on the bed looking at the photograph of Marlene, her face sadder than I'd ever seen it. What was she thinking about? Marlene, of course. What was she wishing? That sweet little Marlene was here to bring her tea? Nothing I did mattered anymore. I took a step backward, moving even more quietly than I'd come, and emptied the cup of tea into the sink.

Dad had gone back into his studio. I went out and asked him if I could go meet Clemmie coming from school.

He turned from his easel. "Good idea, love."

"Is it OK if we stay out for a while and roller-skate?" I didn't mention that I wanted to mail my letters.

"Another good idea," Dad said. He meant roller-skating. "And Susie, go ahead and talk to Clemmie about this if you want. It might make you feel better. And I don't think it's going to make any difference now."

I nodded. It didn't make any difference now because we knew already. We had to wait for the test results to make it official, but we knew anyway.

I got my skates and sat on the front steps to lace them on. Douglas Dog came over, and when I got up and skated he ran beside me as far as the corner, then turned. Douglas doesn't venture too far from home. Smart dog. Lucky dog.

The mailbox was on the next block. I dropped the letters through the slot. How many days to Italy? Too many. How many till Grandpa Lucas visited Kansas City? Even more.

I stared at the houses and yards as I skated past. It was as though I was seeing them for the first time, or maybe the last. The hummingbird feeder shaped like a red apple in the Rodriguezes' window. The funny wooden duck with wings that went up and down when a breeze blew. I'd always thought that duck was the dumbest thing, but now it looked pretty good. My throat was tight with tears.

There was Clemmie walking with Glenda and Lois Hilgartner. She'd probably walk home with them every day after I'd gone. They waved and I waved back and skated faster. Glenda and Lois had to turn off on Duder Street, and as soon as they did Clemmie stopped and faced me.

"Well? The Big Worry? What is it?"

"The Big Worry is that I'm probably not my mom and dad's real daughter," I said.

Her mouth dropped open. "What . . . ?"

I turned my toes in so my skates wouldn't roll away from me and told her the bare bones of what had happened, the two of us just standing there on the corner of Duder and Celeste Streets, standing in the sun.

"You're serious!" Clemmie said.

We began moving slowly toward home.

"Ask your mom if you can come out and skate," I said. "But don't tell her anything about this."

"I won't," Clemmie said meekly, and she shuffled up the steps to her front door, dragging her book bag, giving me a few dazed glances over her shoulder.

Unhappy as I was, it made me smile a little. I'd never seen Clemmie meek or dazed. I'd never seen her shuffle.

We didn't talk as we sidewalk-skated down Continental and onto Westcliff Drive. We crossed at the crossing, and there was the ocean, wild and stormy the way it always is here, smashing itself against the bottom of the cliffs. We stood by the lighthouse, leaning across the railing by the warning sign put there by the SURFERS AGAINST DROWNING. Every year someone climbs over the railing here and the cliff crumbles. Or a mammoth wave comes and the person is never seen again.

Clemmie stooped to loosen one of her skate laces. "You think you're *her*, don't you?"

"I have this feeling," I said. "And then there's the eyebrow thing." I touched the place where the fairy's wand had marked me. "Mr. Stobbel has one, too."

Clemmie shivered. "Weird. Are you going to keep calling him Mr. Stobbel?"

I shrugged. "I don't know. I don't know anything."

"What are you going to do?" Clemmie asked.

"I'm waiting for the tests. If they show I'm for sure not me, I might run away. I'm thinking about it."

"Don't," Clemmie said. "Remember we ran away before? Remember how scary it was when it got dark? Remember how cold, and remember those guys who came up to us and how we ran and . . ."

"But we were only in third grade. And this is almost summer. It's warmer. And I know more."

Clemmie shook her head. "It would be just as scary. Worse, because you'd be alone. And where could you go anyway? If you're going to run away, you'd better wait till you're eighteen or so."

"I've written to my grandparents," I said. "Maybe they'll come through. Of course they may not even be my grandparents anymore. They may not care."

We watched a surfer riding a wave way below us. It looked as if he'd crash into the rocks, but at the last second he pulled a turn and was safe astride his board and heading out to sea again.

"You know what?" Clemmie said. "I wouldn't be surprised if the same thing happened to me. I bet I was switched at birth too." Her eyes were wide and astonished. "Why didn't I think of it before? I'm not a bit like the rest of my family." She spread her hands. "Do you think Sophia and I could be real sisters? I mean it. She's slim and gorgeous and . . . and exotic. I'm ordinary and pudgy and . . ."

"You are not," I told her. "And you look exactly like your mom."

"Thanks a lot!" Clemmie made a face as if I'd insulted her. Honestly, I thought. Clemmie can't stand being left out of anything, even when it's this bad. Can't she at least concentrate on me for once? I guess Clemmie must have been thinking the same thing because she said: "Naw . . . I'm just being overdramatic. My mom says I'm overly dramatic. She is too."

"See?" I said. "Mother and daughter."

We stood quietly leaning on the rail. It was clear enough so we could see Monterey and the big chimneys of the Moss Landing power plant across the bay.

"I'll miss you so much if you have to go, Susan," Clemmie said at last. "Do you think we'll ever see each other again?"

"I doubt it," I said. "They'll probably not let me. They're so mean and horrible. Mom and Dad are kissing up to them, though, hoping for their 'good will.' Yuk!"

"Course, you don't know anything for sure yet, do you?" Clemmie said. "My dad says you should never count your chickens till they're hatched, or your artichokes till they're harvested."

"I know."

"Maybe one of those baby boys belonged to the Stobbels? Didn't you say there were three boys born that night at the hospital?"

"Yes. But I think they know it was a girl."

"Well, maybe they won't like you and they'll send you back. Or, hey! Maybe the blood people made a mistake. I mean, if a whole hospital can make a mistake . . ."

I nodded. "That's true. But you want to hear something awful, Clemmie? I think my mom is more upset that Marlene's dead than she is about losing me."

"Susan!" Clemmie was horrified.

"It's true. If it was just an exchange . . . if they got her for me, they'd probably not be upset at all. Good thing Marlene's . . ." I stopped, just in time. I'd almost said that awful, horrible, ugly thought that had popped into my head when I'd seen Mom lying on the bed, looking at Marlene's picture. I sniffed and fished around in my pocket for a Kleenex.

Clemmie moved so her shoulder touched mine. "Of course they want to keep you. They love you."

She probably didn't know how rotten I was. I hoped Mom and Dad didn't know either.

"We'd better go," I said. "It's getting late."

The next day was Friday. Dad doesn't have classes on Friday, and Mom called in sick, which was no lie. I said I wasn't going to school. At first Mom argued in a halfhearted sort of way, but Dad said: "Oh honey, let her stay home. Would you want to go to school if you were in her place?"

I was glad of the chance to stay home and think, because Clemmie had said something important yesterday, something I hadn't picked up on at the time, and I'd been going over and over it since. "Maybe they won't like you and they'll send you back," she'd said. Well, maybe I could *make* them not like me. How about that? It would sure be better than letting them all push me around.

42

When the phone rang at five minutes past ten, we were all there, Mom and Dad and I.

It was Dad who answered. Dad who murmured, "Thank you. Yes. I understand." It was Dad who looked desperately at Mom, then turned to me. "Oh, honey—I don't know how to tell you this." He gathered me into his arms. "The results are in."

"I didn't turn out to be green," I said. My mouth was numb, as if I'd been sucking on an ice cube. "That's it, isn't it? I'm their color?"

Mom had her arms wrapped around herself as if she was holding her insides together. "What's going to happen next?"

"The lawyers want a joint meeting, all of them, us and the Stobbels," Dad said. "I guess there'll be decisions made then."

I stared at him. Decisions!

It's funny about an earthquake. Even when you know it's coming, there's no way to really prepare yourself. When the hammer falls, it smashes just as hard.

Chapter 6

All day long the phone rang.

"Lawyers, lawyers, lawyers," Dad said. He had a wild, desperate look about him each time he took a call.

"What it comes to is this," he said. "They're all in agreement that we should talk."

"Me too?" I asked.

"No, honey. You don't have to be at the meeting. Be glad about that."

He looked at Mom. "We decided on the same hotel in San Francisco where we met with the Stobbels before. Is that OK?"

Mom nodded.

The same hotel where they'd met with them before. That must have been the time Clemmie and I had thought they were off on a passionate weekend. Didn't I wish!

"They'd like to meet with Susan afterward," Dad said. "Just the five of us, for dinner, for a friendly meal."

Mom and I were sitting side by side on the couch, and I clutched at her hand. "Do I have to? I can't."

"Oh Susie! I know it's hard for you. But it will have to happen sooner or later."

"Later then," I said. "Oh please, no. Don't make me." Then I had another awful thought. "They're not taking me away, are they? Not then?" I was beginning to feel sick.

Dad came over to sit cross-legged on the floor in front of us. Light came in through the miniblind and made bars of silver across his face. "Susan, listen to me. No arrangements have been worked out yet. Nobody's taking you anywhere. The Stobbels want to meet you. That's all. It's understandable. We'll be with you."

"Can I sit between you and Mom?"

"Yes, of course you can. We're all going to be under a lot of strain, but we have to make an effort. None of us wants this to go before a judge. There's no telling which way a judge would jump. He might decide for the biological parents all the way."

"The what?" I asked.

"For them. On the other hand, he might say you

45

would be better off staying with us. We don't know, Susie. That's the problem. That's one of the reasons we want to try settling things out of court. An arrangement where we share . . . where we get to have you for part of the time and they . . ."

"I don't *want* them to have me for part of the time. I live here. I've always lived here." I couldn't help adding, "Don't you want me anymore? Don't you?"

"Honey!" Mom put her arms around me. "We want you more than anything in the world. Your dad and I have to help work things out. You have to help."

I didn't answer.

She left her arm around my shoulder as she asked Dad, "What time on Monday?"

"Two in the afternoon. The lawyers have to fly up from L.A. The Stobbels, I think, come on a different flight. They leave from John Wayne Airport."

"John Wayne Airport," I repeated. "Is that really its name?"

"I think I'll book a room in the hotel for Monday night," Dad said. "Then we won't have to drive home after dinner. And Susan will have a place to wait comfortably while we have our meeting."

"Will you tell me what they say, Dad? If they decide things about me, I want to know. Promise you'll tell."

"I promise," Dad said.

"Monday at two?" Mom asked in a dazed sort of

way. "What time is it now?"

"It's twelve twenty . . . Friday," Dad told her gently, and Mom said, "Oh, it's going to be a long weekend."

Maybe it was to make time pass or to get away from the phone or to get away from ourselves and our thoughts that we drove out to Davenport on Saturday morning. Davenport is where we go to watch the whales migrate. In fall they are on their way south to Mexico to give birth to their babies. In spring they start the long swim back to Alaska. People say that when the new babies get tired, the mothers carry them on their backs. I'd never seen that. This wasn't whale migrating season. We stood on the cliffs looking out across the empty sea and Mom kept asking Dad what time it was.

Once he sighed and told her it was still Saturday, but not in a mean way, more as if he was really sorry to have to tell her that. I couldn't figure out if she wanted time to pass more quickly or more slowly. We stood for a bit longer and I was wondering if whale babies ever got mixed up. If sometimes a mother swam all those thousands of miles carrying her baby on her back and when she got to Alaska some other whale would stop her and say: "Hey! You've got the wrong calf. There was a mix-up way back in Mexico."

No, I thought. Whale mothers probably knew the

touch and smell and sounds of their own babies.

"What time is it?" Mom asked, shivering. "Maybe we'd better just go home."

"Yes," I said. "Let's go home."

And Dad said, "Let's. And how about if I fix dinner?"

He was at the stove, stirring the angel-hair pasta, when the doorbell rang. I went to answer it, first looking out the living room window to check on who was there. One of those postal trucks with a big eagle on the side was parked at our curb.

I opened the door.

"Susan Moretti?" the man asked.

"For me?" I asked.

He grinned. "If you're Susan Moretti."

I nodded. It couldn't be an answer from Italy or Kansas City yet. Sometimes I get letters or cards from Grandma and Grandpa and Aunt Lissa even when it's not my birthday or Christmas, and once Grandpa Lucas had sent me some sandstone roses from Oklahoma when he was on one of his trips. They'd crumbled to dust by the time I got them. I never told him. But this letter seemed extra important and I began to get excited. Maybe it was from one of them. What else could it be? I signed where the mailman pointed, and he pulled off one of the labels and gave me the big envelope with the eagle on the front.

"What on earth?" I asked, and he said, "Beats me," grinned again and went back to his truck.

"Mom!" I called. "Dad!" And then I saw the return address:

> BARBARA STOBBEL
> 3252 Nims Road
> Laguna Niguel, CA

"Mom!" I yelled real loud. "It's from *her*." I let go of the envelope so it dropped at my feet and rubbed my hands along the legs of my jeans. I wanted to bawl. Not from *her*.

Mom picked up the envelope.

"Susan. Please. Remember what we said about facing up to things? How you must do your part, too? This isn't going to bite you. Open it."

"I can't."

"Yes you can. Here, take it."

Dad had come over, too. He was still carrying the long pasta spoon with the little holes in it.

He turned on the table lamp.

"Sit down, Susie."

The envelope was well stuck and hard to open. Inside was a blue letter-sized envelope. "Susan Moretti" was written across the front in big, round letters. I looked up pleadingly at Dad.

"Yes," he said. "You have to open that one, too. But you can be by yourself if you'd rather."

"No. No. You and Mom stay. Please."

Behind him on the stove the water boiled over in the pasta pot and there was that quick hissing and sudden singed smell. I waited while he went to lift it off.

There were two sheets of blue paper.

"Should I read it out loud?" I asked.

"Whatever way you want." Mom's voice was so calm, so ordinary, but I saw the way she shaded her eyes from the lamplight and the bulge of the purple vein on her forehead. Headache, I thought. Bad one. She's not going to mention it though.

I read aloud:

"Dear Susan:
I can't imagine how difficult this must be for you. It's difficult for all of us, but for you it must be worse."

I stopped, flipped to the second page, looked at the end of the letter and said, "I was scared she might have signed it 'Mother,' but she didn't." I glanced quickly at Mom's pale, thin face, then went back to the letter.

"I'm sending this so I can say things to you before we meet. I want you to know that

Harry and I will do everything we can to
help you through this. You have been very
blessed in the mother and father you have
had for the past 12 years. They've loved and
cared for you . . ."

I stopped because the words swam in front of my
eyes and my nose was dripping. "Does anyone have a
tissue?" I asked, and Mom found a wad of unused
ones in her sweater pocket, passed me some and kept
some for herself.

"Pass one here," Dad said, and he blew his nose and
wiped his eyes too.

"They've loved and cared for you, and we
want to make this as easy for them as we
possibly can,"

I read.

"Easy," Mom said. *"Easy?"*

Dad reached across and patted her knee. "Mrs.
Stobbel doesn't mean it that way, honey. She's trying
to be nice."

"I know from what they've told me what a
dear girl you are. We love you already. How
could we not? You are our child, and in the

51

end that means everything. Harry and I are looking forward to being with you if only, initially, for a short, get-acquainted time."

I read that last sentence again silently, then looked at Dad. "Doesn't 'initially' mean 'at first'? She's saying it's going to be just a short time at first on Monday at dinner, and then . . . after that . . ."

"Sh, honey," Dad said. "We know they're going to want to be with you a lot. That's why they started all this in the first place. If they didn't want you, they'd have let it go."

"It's natural that you should resent us for a while for changing your life so drastically. But Susan, try to see it from our point of view. Through no fault of ours we lost you. Now we've found you. We can offer you a loving home and loving parents, too. And a small brother. He's only four, so you can imagine how confusing this is for him. Marlene's death hit him hard, but he is as anxious to meet his new big sister as we are to meet our new, but always, daughter.
Fondest love . . .
Harry and Barbara Stobbel"

_____

Underneath, in raggedy red crayon, was printed JEREMY with three X's next to it.

I put the letter back in the envelope and set it beside me on the couch. Then I got up and stumbled across the living room. I heard Mom start to come after me. I heard Dad say quietly, "Amanda, let her be. She needs to be by herself for a while."

I went straight to my little house, wedged myself through the door and sat in the warm, known dark. Maybe I would never, never come out.

Chapter 7

We got to San Francisco at ten after twelve with lots of time to check into the hotel room before Mom and Dad's meeting. All three of us were jumpy and nervous, and once Dad even said to Mom, "I explained all that to you before. I wish you'd just listen!" and then he said, "Sorry, honey. I know it's hard to concentrate on anything today."

Before they left me in the room, they wrote down the extension number of where they'd be downstairs if I needed to get them. They gave me the usual warning about not opening the door, and Dad showed me that he'd hung a PLEASE DO NOT DISTURB sign on the outside handle. They said there was a women's tennis match on cable sports and asked two or three times if I had my book. Dad got me ice from the ice machine and a diet Pepsi and a little package of nuts.

"Is there anything else you might want?" Mom asked.

"To go home."

"Oh honey, that will come, too," she said. "I promise."

"How long will you be at the meeting?"

Mom glanced at Dad. "It might take a while. I don't think we'll be back till four thirty or five. The lawyers will probably have papers to sign and heaven knows what." She nodded toward my little overnight bag. "Hang up your dress, will you, love, so it won't get creased."

I nodded. Big deal if it got creased!

The room seemed empty when they'd gone. It was cold, too, with the air conditioner too high, but I couldn't find how to turn it down. I prowled around, sitting on their queen-sized bed, then on my double.

Down below, in the room that was extension number 1512, they were talking about me, deciding what would happen.

The tennis match was one-sided and boring. I kept forgetting which player was which. I couldn't concentrate to read. I prowled some more. There was stationery in a drawer and postcards with a view of the pool and the hotel gardens. I wrote a card to Clemmie and one to Grandma and Grandpa Moretti.

"Dear Clemmie, I wish you were here."

"Dear Grandma and Grandpa, Did you get my letter? I love you." But there were no stamps, so I left both cards in the drawer.

Down below, at extension 1512, they'd be signing those agreements.

At five o'clock I called. A woman answered. "Yes?"

Behind her I could hear a low hum of conversation.

"May I speak to Mrs. Moretti, please?"

A pause. Then she said, "Certainly." She'd be gesturing to Mom. "I think it's Susan."

"Susan?" Mom asked.

"I was wondering when you'd be finished," I said.

"We're almost through. Why don't you go ahead and shower and get dressed. Your dad and I won't need to change."

I lowered my voice. "What did you decide?"

"We can talk about that later, love. I have to go now. See you in a few minutes."

She hung up the phone.

On the TV the two tennis players still raced around the court. I turned them off and went to get ready.

"You look very nice," Mom said as soon as they came in. "I'm glad we had that dress." The dress was cream-colored heavy cotton with a lace collar and pleats down the front. Dad had said it was a Gainsborough dress and he approved. Mom and I'd bought it last March when he'd had a one-man art exhibit up at the college. We'd bought the cream-colored tights to go with it and the shoes with the bows in front. This was only the second time I'd worn any of them. I had goose bumps on my arm from being nervous and being cold. I tried to rub them away while Mom fluffed up my hair.

"That last cut, whatever it was, has grown out so nicely," she said. "You're very pretty, sweetheart."

"Sure," I said. "And I have to look pretty for the Stobbels."

"I expect they'll love you whatever way you look, just as we do," Mom said seriously.

I didn't like the way that sounded. Too reasonable. Too friendly.

"You said you'd tell me what happened."

Dad glanced at his watch. "We have a little time. Barbara and Harry made reservations in the hotel restaurant for six thirty. They have to catch a plane home at ten."

I was stunned. "*Barbara* and *Harry*? How lovely."

Dad didn't seem to hear me. "They're coming here to the room to pick us up at six. We thought it would be easier for the three of you to meet for the first time in this setting rather than in a restaurant."

I glanced wildly around. "*Here*? At six?"

"Let's sit down," Dad said gently.

57

He sat on the edge of my double bed and patted the place beside him. Mom took the big, overstuffed chair opposite us, and Dad held my hand, twining his fingers through mine.

"First, Susie, I want you to understand that your mom and I and Harry and Barbara are trying to do what's best for you. We don't know yet what that is. We'll make mistakes, but for now we've made the most sensible arrangements we can think of."

"Go on." His wedding band cut into my finger as he squeezed my hand but I didn't try to ease it.

"We agreed that you should go to Laguna Niguel next weekend, just for two days. Just to get acclimatized."

"Just to get what?" It was so cold. I wished I could climb under the bedcover.

"To let you see what it's like there. What they're like."

"You agreed to that?" The words came with big spaces between them. "You . . . agreed . . . to . . . that?"

"Your mom and I will be going too. They understood our need to be with you. We have to see the kind of home you'll have and how it will be for you. We'll all go and we'll all come back."

My legs started to shake. I curled my toes hard inside my shoes. "After that? After the weekend?"

"The legal arrangements are that you'll be with us till school ends, the last week in June. Then you'll go to them until the beginning of August. August, you'll come back and spend with us." Dad looked away. He seemed to have run out of words.

"I still say we should get her more often," Mom began. "It's not fair. They—"

"Sh," Dad said. "We've been all through that, Amanda."

Mom turned away, blew her nose, turned back to me. "In fall you'll start school down there," she said. "We'll come visit you anytime you like, and you can come back for weekends and for part of spring vacation. And then we'll take turns with Thanksgiving and Christmas each year." She gave Dad a "help-me" glance. "But all this depends on how . . . on how you adjust," she went on. "If it's too awful for you, we have the right . . ."

"But don't forget, Amanda, they have the right too," Dad interrupted. I could see something moving in his throat, something the size of a Ping-Pong ball.

How could they go along with all this? It must be because of Marlene. I remembered the way Mom had looked at Marlene's picture.

"You are our child, and in the end that means everything." Someone had said that. Who had said it? Mom was smiling at me now. None of this mattered to her.

59

She didn't care, just sitting there, plucking at her skirt, making little pouches in it, damp and spotty.

"Didn't you fight for me?" I asked. "Didn't you?" I was screaming. "If *I* had a daughter and somebody tried to take her away I'd . . . I'd . . . But then I'm not, am I? I'm not your daughter."

I jumped off the bed, and Dad stood, too, so we were facing each other.

"Barbara and Harry and your mom and I have to cooperate on this, Susan," he said. "If we don't, it's going to be even harder. And heaven knows it's hard enough."

"It doesn't seem hard for you. Not a bit. You and Mom and Barbara and Harry! You're just so palsy-walsy!"

"Susan! This is killing us," Mom said, and I saw that she'd risen, too, one hand holding on to the bedside table as if she might fall down. "Don't you know it's killing us?"

"No. I don't know that: I don't!"

I ran into the bathroom, locked the door and leaned against it.

Now they were tapping on it.

"Susan? Susan? Come out, sweetheart." That was Dad.

"No."

"We have a lot more to tell you if you'll just come

out. Please, love." Mom's voice cracked, and I imagined it like our big Hopi pot during the earthquake, quivering into little pieces.

I stared at myself in the mirror. Things, words, jumbled together in my head. The dinner tonight, then the weekend, then more than a month, and then—forever. In the mirror my mouth was twisted and open, like a clown's, and my eyes were watering.

"Come on, love," Dad called. "It's not going to be so bad. It can't be that terrible to have two sets of parents who love you. We'll work on getting more time with you, but this is an OK start, isn't it?"

"It's not OK. I don't want two sets of parents." I squinched up my eyes and scowled at myself. That horrible eyebrow that was just like *his*. That was the worst!

Dad's old black-leather toilet bag sat on the bathroom counter. I opened it and peered inside. Maybe they heard the small sound the zipper made as I slid it across.

"Susan? What are you doing? Open the door." Mom's voice had an edge of something in it. Fear maybe.

Dad had brought a couple of those orange-and-white plastic razors. I took one out. His shaving brush is stubby and worn, and he has a mug of soap with a screw-on lid. I'd gotten him this one for his birthday,

61

and already the soap was hollow in the middle. I knew how to shave. I'd watched him lots of times edging the razor carefully around his mustache, winking at me in the mirror. I like watching him. My insides hurt now, just thinking about it. I ran the hot water over the brush, soaped my right eyebrow and with a few scratchy strokes took it off.

"This has gone on long enough. Open the door this minute, Susan, or you're in big trouble," Dad yelled.

There was soap in my eye, stinging like crazy. Where my eyebrow had been stung too. I wiped at it with the washcloth, blinked hard, and looked at myself. I hadn't thought taking off such a little thing would make me look this weird. It wasn't as if I had big hairy clunkers that you'd miss a lot. Who'd have thought you'd notice it this much? How could I be so suddenly lopsided? Maybe it would be better if . . .

I soaped up the other eyebrow and took it off too.

"What are you doing in there, Susan?" Mom's voice quavered. "Please don't do anything silly."

"We're going to call housekeeping." That was Dad again. "They'll have a way to get that door open. Answer me, Susan."

I couldn't. I was peering at my bald face in the mirror. Oh, I looked ugly.

"I am counting to ten, Susan," Dad called. "And I warn you, if you don't open this door . . ."

I opened it on seven.

Mom gasped.

"For heaven's sake, Susan," Dad said, and I'd never heard him so angry. "What do you think you're doing, scaring us like that?"

And then Mom said: "Oh honey, why did you have to do that?"

"At least I don't look like *him* anymore," I said.

"Oh yes, you do, Susan." Mom's voice was so sad and tired.

The three of us were just standing there in this awful silence when someone knocked on the door.

"I think they're here," Dad said.

Chapter 8

Dad opened the door. I heard a woman say: "We weren't sure if we should knock or not." And I was all at once so nervous, I could have thrown up. "There's a DO NOT DISTURB sign on the door handle," she added.

"Sorry," Dad said. "I forgot to take it off. Come in, please."

In another second I'd be face to face with them. I wanted to hide behind Mom's skirt, the way little kids do when a stranger appears.

The Stobbels paused just inside the room, and I was looking at them for the first time, at the ones who were supposed to be my true parents.

In one glance I saw that she was very fat and very pretty with a mass of soft dark hair. Her dress was a flowered print, sleeveless and loose. And he had a beard. Nobody had told me that. It wasn't the big Santa Claus kind of beard or the wimpy wispy kind. His was short, and neat and curly. He was stork tall, stork thin. Nobody had prepared me for the way he stood, one hand in his jacket pocket, slouched forward the way I slouch. I almost said "Don't droop, Mr. Stobbel" in the voice Mom and Dad use when they say that to me.

"Hello, Susan." Mrs. Stobbel sounded as if she might cry any minute. They were both moving toward me now. They wouldn't hug and kiss me, would they? I'd die.

Mrs. Stobbel put out her hand and took mine, and I thought she was going to shake it, which would have been weird, too, but instead she held on to it. I made mine as limp as a wet sock. "Susan," she said. "Susan."

Mr. Stobbel was smiling, his teeth gleaming white through his beard. "We're so glad we found you," he said.

Mrs. Stobbel's lips trembled. "And you're so tall and pretty." I knew I had to say something, but I couldn't, and when words did come out, they were so stupid I couldn't believe them.

"Usually I have eyebrows," I said.

"I did notice they weren't there." She sounded worried. "What happened, sweetheart?"

Sweetheart! Still, the checker in Vons calls me

sweetheart. No need to feel this little lump of panic. . . .
I eased my hand from hers. "I shaved them off."

"Is the no-eyebrow look 'in' now in Santa Cruz?"
Mr. Stobbel's voice was soft, maybe because it had to
come out through his beard. Crazy that Mom had said
he looked like me. How could she tell? She'd meant
only the one eyebrow, and I'd fixed that.

"No. It's not the 'in' look," I said, surly as could be.

"If they don't like you maybe they'll send you
back." that's what Clemmie had said. If they didn't
like me, maybe they wouldn't even *take* me.

Beside me I heard Dad inviting them to sit down,
saying he'd planned on having room service bring up
coffee but we'd had a small crisis and he hadn't gotten
around to it.

They all sat, and after Dad gave me one of his looks,
I sat too.

Mrs. Stobbel had her hands folded in her lap. Her
right hand kept pulling on her left, moving along as if
counting the fingers to make sure they were still in
place.

"You got my letter?" she asked.

"Your mother really worried over what she should
say," Mr. Stobbel added, and I glared at Mom.

"You *knew* Mrs. Stobbel was going to write to me?"

Mom's face had gone pink and her voice trembled.
"Susan, he doesn't mean . . ."

66

"Harry!" Mrs. Stobbel cracked one of her fingers, loud as gum popping. The sound made me jump.

"Gee, I'm sorry. I forgot." Mr. Stobbel shook his head. "I didn't mean to say 'your *mother*.' I meant to say Barbara worried over what she should say in the letter. Not your mom. It's . . . it's just confusing, you know."

"It's horrible." I pointed at Mom. "*She's* my mother. She'll always be my mother. She's the only mother I've got." Tears trickled miserably down my face.

"Sh," Mom whispered. "Don't cry, sweetheart. Please don't. If you do, I'll start too, and I'm trying so hard . . . so hard."

I pointed to Dad. "And he'll always be my father. Always."

"We know that. We understand," Mr. Stobbel said.

Dad came over and put his hand on the top of my head, the way he does sometimes. "It's OK, sweetheart. Everything's just too much for all of us."

In the silence I heard the sharp crack of another of Mrs. Stobbel's fingers.

"Well." Dad smiled a phony smile. "It's a little early, but perhaps we should just go on down to the restaurant. They can probably seat us."

Everyone quickly stood up again.

"We do appreciate the chance to meet Susan in private, though." Mr. Stobbel took his wife's hand, maybe to stop her pulling her fingers right out of their sockets or maybe to comfort her. "It was certainly better . . . wasn't it, honey?"

Mrs. Stobbel didn't answer. She might have been thinking what I was thinking—that it couldn't have been much worse.

It was so early, the restaurant was almost empty.

I sat between Mom and Dad at a round table that had a pink cloth and pink napkins that stood up like fans in stemmed water glasses. Candles flickered.

We ordered from the menus, but when the food came, no one seemed interested.

The Stobbels asked about the earthquake, and if we'd been OK. They asked about Mom's and Dad's jobs at the university, and Mrs. Stobbel said: "My, you must both be very clever," in an admiring way. Dad asked about the Med fly problem and if their drought situation down there was as bad as ours up north. And after that there was this awful silence where no one could think of anything else to say.

I took a bite of salad. The lettuce was the bitter kind that I hate.

Mr. Stobbel coughed. "I suppose it's all right to talk about today's procedures in front of Susan?"

"We tell Susan everything," Mom said stiffly. "After all, she's the one most affected."

Mr. Stobbel nodded. "We try to be open with our children, too. I mean . . . now . . . with Jeremy." He folded his napkin though all his food was still uneaten, and spread his hands on the pink cloth, one on each side of the plate.

"I'm glad we got an out-of-court agreement. It's infinitely better for Susan. Anything we can do to make it less traumatic for her is a plus."

I spit out my piece of chewed-up lettuce, all stringy and yukko, and looked to make sure they'd noticed. No one had, not even Mom, who notices anything gross at the table. Too bad.

I slid my tongue across the bitterness on my teeth.

"Susan?" Dad said. "We didn't have time to tell you this before Harry and Barbara came. We found out today that there's going to be quite a lot of money held in trust for you till you're eighteen."

"You mean, the hospital's sorry they made a mistake and they're paying me money? I'll be rich?" I asked.

"Something like that," Dad said. "And you'll only be pretty rich. So don't go getting uppity on us." His grin was forced.

With my hands under the table I counted on my fingers how many years and months it would be till I was eighteen. If the Stobbel's thought they could hang on to me after I became rich, they were crazy. Then I noticed how Mrs. Stobbel had her hands under the table, probably working on her fingers too, so brought mine up into sight. I sure didn't want her to think I'd inherited any of *her* habits! Five years and four months to go. I'd never be able to stick it out.

Every now and then I'd feel the Stobbels staring at me. When our glances met, they'd smile.

"That's such a pretty dress," Mrs. Stobbel told me.

"Thank you. My mother bought it for me for a very special occasion, didn't you, Mom?" And I gave her a quick peck on the cheek to show the Stobbels how close and loving we were, and to make them feel left out. But Mom's look told me she knew what I was up to.

I was watching the Stobbels secretly too. Could these two people really be my parents? They were so different in every way from Mom and Dad. The way they dressed . . . Mom in her dark print skirt and stockings, her low-heeled shoes. Santa Cruz style. Mrs. Stobbel across from her, smooth and tanned and plump, bursting with color. Mr. Stobbel, lanky and somehow graceful, beside Dad, small and intense and rumpled. So different in every way.

There was another uncomfortable silence. Dad broke it by pointing to a framed Georgia O'Keeffe painting on the wall and asking if by any chance they'd seen the O'Keeffe exhibit in Los Angeles. The Stobbels turned to inspect the print, then shook their heads. Mr. Stobbel said they hardly ever drove up to

L.A., not if they could help it. He said the traffic was terrible and getting worse. And to be honest, they weren't too interested in museums.

I sniffed and said under my breath: "That figures."

Dad frowned at me, but unfortunately I think he was the only one who heard. I'd tried to say it loudly enough, but it's hard to be rude, even on purpose. Lots of people are, though, and I decided I could be if I worked at it.

Mrs. Stobbel said they sometimes drove up to catch a Lakers game at the Forum. Or once a year to go to the boat show. They loved sailing.

She asked me if I liked sports and I shrugged. I like some sports, but I wasn't going to tell *her* anything.

Dad said he understood Mr. Stobbel was in the swimming-pool business, and Mr. Stobbel said yes, they were kept very busy, and Barbara managed the books and sent out the bills and he didn't know what he would do without her. There was a lot of tenderness in his voice and in the way he looked at her.

I listened to the talk. How weird it was. Like a dream, almost. Who were these people? Why were we having dinner with them?

And then Mrs. Stobbel said: "Marlene was a very good swimmer. She was on the team at the Y and she won quite a few trophies. This summer she . . . she was going to go to swimming camp."

71

Mom took a sip of water. From under the tabletop came the faint crack-crack-cracking of Mrs. Stobbel's knuckles.

"Oh, I almost forgot." She lifted her large straw purse, opened it, took a small package wrapped in speckled tissue paper sprinkled with stars and held it across to me. "Jeremy sent you this."

"Oh." I took it, pushed aside my dinner plate and began peeling off the Scotch tape. It looked as if Jeremy had used a whole roll of the stuff. Inside was a small bulky something carefully wrapped in still more tissue.

I glanced at Mom. Her smile was strained and her eyes narrowed. Pain, I thought. Headache again. No wonder.

When I stripped away the last of the paper, I found a green tin alligator about the size of one of the small bars of soap in the hotel bathroom. Its mouth was wide open to show its pointed tin teeth, and a wind-up key stuck out of its tail end.

"It's Jeremy's favorite toy," Mrs. Stobbel said. "He's had it since he was two. It floats, and he can take it in the pool, or in the tub."

Mr. Stobbel smiled. "Once he almost lost it in the ocean and I just about drowned getting it back. Didn't I, Barbara? Remember?"

She nodded and leaned across to touch the key. I

noticed what pretty hands she had, the fingers long and slim, not like the rest of her. They probably got that way from pulling on them. She had on red nail polish. I'd never seen Mom wear red nail polish in my life.

"When you wind it up, it goes dashing around on top of the water, snapping its jaws," she said.

I held the alligator in the palm of my hand. Its black beady eyes looked past me to the other side of the dining room. This was from my little brother. My little brother. I said the words again inside my head, waiting to feel something. I didn't feel a thing. Jeremy was as unreal as everything else.

I rewrapped the alligator in a layer of tissue. "Will you please tell him thank you," I said.

"You can tell him yourself, next weekend." Mr. Stobbel looked nervously at Dad and raised one of his eyebrows. The one like I used to have. "Susan *does* know you're all coming for the weekend?"

"Yes."

Mom quietly fingered a pill from her little pill box. I knew she only took one of those things when her headache was really bad.

"Let us know what time your plane gets in and we'll meet you, Jim," Mr. Stobbel said.

"Thanks. We appreciate that."

Nobody wanted dessert. The Stobbels ordered coffee, black, and Dad and Mom ordered cappuccino.

"Can I have one, Dad?" I asked.

Dad help up three fingers to the waiter. "Sure. Make that three cappuccinos."

But at exactly the same second Mrs. Stobbel said: "Susan? Cappuccino? You're too . . ."

She stopped in mid-sentence.

"How many cappuccinos do I bring?" the waiter asked in an impatient hoity-toity way.

"I'm sorry I interfered," Mrs. Stobbel said. "It's just, cappuccino seems so . . ."

"No. No." That was Dad. "If you think Susan shouldn't . . ." He floundered helplessly. "Since we were in Italy last year visiting her grandparents, we've allowed her to have one on a special occasion, but . . ."

"Of course. Certainly." Mr. Stobbel tilted his head back to look up at the waiter. "Two coffees. Three cappuccinos."

I sat there, mad as could be. Who did these people think they were, bossing me around, telling Dad what I could and couldn't have? As if he hadn't been taking care of me for twelve years? As if he didn't know best? A small voice inside my head said, "They think they're your *parents*, that's who. And they are. They can say no to cappuccino or anything else from now on."

I couldn't believe it when a big, hiccupy sob exploded out of me. It was so loud that the couple at the next table looked over. The young guy said, all fake serious, "Drunk again, huh!" and grinned.

I lifted Jeremy's alligator and pushed back my chair. "Could I please be excused now and go back to the room?"

Mom apologized. "She's tired."

Mr. Stobbel glanced at his watch. "Let's just skip all the coffees and go. Barbara and I need to get to the airport."

"You'll be way too early," Dad told him. "Do you want to come up with us . . ." He let the less-than-enthusiastic words drift away.

"Thanks, but we won't. We like to get to airports in plenty of time."

There was some business stuff about the bill and then we were all in the lobby, standing around awkwardly.

"Good-bye, Susan," Mrs. Stobbel said.

"We'll see you next week," Mr. Stobbel added. I had a feeling they were holding back, being careful. Thank goodness. No mushy stuff—just "Good-bye, Susan."

The adults shook hands and I thought, it's over for now. Relief. They've gone.

But then Mrs. Stobbel looked at Mom and said in

the saddest, saddest voice: "I wish you could have known Marlene. She was the sweetest girl. I've been thinking about that all night. I know it's impossible, but I just wish you could have known her." Tears ran silently down her face. "We loved her so much."

She and Mom both took a step forward, and suddenly they had their arms around each other and they were both sobbing, holding on to each other and sobbing. Mom's head was pressed against Mrs. Stobbel's shoulder, and I heard her whisper: "I would have loved her too. I would have."

They moved apart then, drying their eyes, whispering their good-byes. Somehow I knew there'd been a connection made and understood. The two mothers crying over the lost daughter. Who was crying over me? We stood to watch the Stobbels cross the lobby and leave before we walked silently to the elevators.

As soon as we got to our room, I went in the bathroom. In the mirror my pale, bald rabbit face stared back at me through watery eyes. Where my brows had been were sore-looking red marks with one or two straggly hairs that I'd missed. Ugly, ugly. And they'd probably grow back all bristly. Maybe bushed out, like fur canopies over my eyes. And it hadn't made a bit of difference anyway. They all loved Marlene. But now I was all there was, so the Stobbels would take me, however nasty and ugly I was.

I was still holding Jeremy's package, and I un-wrapped it and filled the washbasin with water, wound the alligator and put him in. I watched him swim round and round in circles, snapping his little jaws and going nowhere.

Chapter 9

When we got home early on Tuesday afternoon, the phone was ringing. Dad answered it and I heard him say: "Oh, hi, Mama. We just got in." Then: "I'm sorry you had to try so many times."

Grandma Moretti calling from Italy! I glanced at the clock. It would be late in Perugia, ten thirty at night. I counted on my fingers how many days since I'd mailed the letter. Maybe she'd gotten it.

"Oh, it went about as well as could be expected," Dad was saying. "Well, Susan *did* have a hard time. But now she has met the Stobbels, so . . ." He paused. "I know, I know. I didn't say it would ever be *easy* for her."

She knows, I thought. Hurrah! Give him heck, Grandma!

Now Dad was sounding exasperated. "Mama, we

can't do that. Why not? Because we've signed legal papers, for one thing. Because our home is here. What kind of life would it be for Susan anyway, hiding all the time, never being able to come back to the United States?" Pause. "That *would* happen. You may think it wouldn't, but it would."

I tugged at his elbow. "I wouldn't mind hiding or . . ."

He nudged me away and said, "Susan, please."

I went past him to the refrigerator and poured myself a glass of milk. Behind me Dad was saying, "We're *not* giving her up. We're sharing her. We have to remember that the Stobbels are decent people. Besides, Mama, do you want us all to go to jail?"

He swung around, drummed his fingers on the counter and said into the phone: "Well, at the very least we'd be ordered back to face charges."

Mom had brought in the mail and was standing close to me, silently sorting it. She handed me a card with a moose on the front. *Just drove the whole length of the Alaska Highway*, Grandpa Lucas wrote. *Saw a few of these big guys on the way*. I felt like bawling. The Alaska Highway! He hadn't been through Kansas City yet, and he was on his way to the North Pole without me. One day he'd pick up his mail or he'd call from some little town in North Dakota or Wyoming, and Mom would say: "Oh, Dad . . . such awful news about Susan!"

I stared out of the kitchen window at our untidy backyard with its overgrown vegetable garden. On the phone I could hear Dad trying to interrupt Grandma Moretti, saying: "Wait, Mama, let me finish." But Grandma Moretti is hard to interrupt or to stop once she gets going.

"No, Mama. It's not a matter of money, but thank you anyway," he was saying. "Don't you know we'd sell everything we possess to fight for Susan if we thought we could win?" He listened.

Outside, a brown squirrel ran along the telephone wires; it jumped to a tree branch, then back to the wires, balancing like a trapeze artist.

Dad sighed loudly. "Mama. Remember the old saying? Half a loaf is better than no bread? Yes, she's here. Yes, you can speak to her, but try not to upset her, OK?" He held the phone toward me.

"It won't upset me. I want to talk to her." I set my glass on the counter.

"Hello, Grandma."

"Susan?" She sounded as close as next door. Too bad she wasn't. She'd be standing in the kitchen of their big apartment on Via Vanucci. She and Grandpa had gone to Italy to find their roots three years ago after Grandpa had had his heart attack and retired. I don't think they found any roots, but they found Perugia and fell in love with it and stayed, and then

80

Aunt Lissa went to live over there too.

"Are you coming for me?" I asked. "Please come."

"Oh honey, I wish we could. I truly wish we could."

"Did you get my letter?"

"You wrote? We didn't get it yet. Your father called before you left for San Francisco. Believe me, if we were younger and your grandpa was well . . ."

She stopped and I imagined her words running along the phone lines, over the Alps and under the ocean, a string of them, balancing like the squirrel, running from her to me. But I had a horrible feeling that only the words were going to be running toward me.

"Your father should be doing *something*! We think he's such a wimp." I covered the phone with my hand. "She thinks you're a wimp," I told Dad, and he shook his head to show how hopeless she was.

"Your grandpa's telling me to butt out," Grandma said. "Here he is."

"Susan?" That was his quiet, calm voice. "How are you, sweetheart?"

"All right, I guess."

"Your grandma and I are going to come to Santa Cruz for the whole month of August so we can be with you."

But not before. They weren't going to rescue me either. I nodded.

81

"Your Aunt Lissa says she loves you and that she's sent you a bottle of Amore perfume. She says be careful how you use it. You could drive the California fellows crazy."

"Tell her thanks," I said.

"Your grandma's pulling the phone out of my hand again. Arrivederci, sweetheart."

"Arrivederci, Grandpa."

There was the sound of faraway whispering.

"Susan? I'm not going to let up on your father. I'll bug him and bug him." Then, for the first time, I heard a tremble in her voice. "Do you know yet if you have other grandparents? I mean, besides us and your Grandpa Lucas?"

"I don't know. Probably."

"Well, don't forget us. Don't forget we love you."

I knew they did. That wasn't the problem. The problem was that they were old and far away, and they didn't honestly think we could win either.

I'd just finished breakfast the next morning when Mom came out of the bathroom and said: "Better get a move on, love, or you'll be late for school."

"I'm not going," I said. "What's the point?" My voice was almost as surly with her as it had been with the Stobbels. All night long I'd been reliving the two of them, Barbara and Amanda, hugging and crying "I loved her" and "I would have loved her, too."

"Next year I'll be going to John Wayne Middle School or something equally gross," I said.

"There are almost two weeks of classes left, Susan, and you are not just going to sit around at home thinking unhappy thoughts." Mom poured coffee beans into the grinder. "Anyway, your dad and I will be at work, so you can't stay here by yourself."

The coffee grinder made its loud, rattling buzz as she turned it on. I raised my voice over the noise. "Everybody at school will know about me," I shouted. "It will be horrible."

Mom didn't answer till she'd switched off the grinder. "No one will know, except Clemmie. The Stobbels, the lawyers, all of us have worked hard to keep a low profile on this. Dad and I will go down and explain the circumstances to Mrs. Ledu on the last day of school."

Mrs. Ledu is our principal. She tells us that nothing in the world could ever surprise her. But she was surprised when Simon Peck put a worm in her jacket pocket. This will surprise her, too.

I looked pleadingly at Mom. Her face was calm, but I'd never seen her eyes so flat and dark. "Just be glad the newspapers haven't heard about it yet," she said.

Dad came in then, all freshly shaved and dressed in his cord jacket and pants and nice checked shirt. It was just like a regular morning—like every morning of my life. But it wasn't.

He stood to examine me, then held up the book he was carrying. "You know, this no-eyebrow thing is interesting. Look!"

His finger marked the page and he flipped the book open on the table. "The *Armada Portrait of Queen Elizabeth I*," he said. "See? No eyebrows. Very regal. Course you need to skin your hair back and wind a few pearls in it and get yourself a humongous ruffle for around your neck." He closed the book and dropped a kiss on the top of my head. "So? How's it going, your majesty?"

I could see he was trying to pretend this *was* just another morning. I didn't smile. "*She* says I have to go to school," I told him.

"If by *she* you mean your mother, she's right."

"But we've decided she isn't my mother," I said. "Mrs. Stobbel is." My mouth dropped open. How could I have said that? Where had it come from? I'd meant to be rude and horrible to the Stobbels, not to Mom and Dad. "I didn't mean it," I wailed. "I didn't."

Mom was standing still as death, her back to me, and I pushed aside my chair, ran across and wound my arms around her. "Mom! Mom! I didn't mean to hurt you. I'm sorry. It's just . . . I've been thinking that

84

probably you're wishing you could have had Marlene always. That she's your real child and you love her more than me even if she's, you know . . ."

Mom turned, and I couldn't even look at her as I buried my face in her hair that was cold and damp and smelling of sassafras shampoo.

"I know you didn't mean to hurt me. And about loving Marlene more than you, that's not true, Susan. Love isn't something that you have so much of, like a candy bar, and when you've shared it out there's none left for anyone else."

She held me away and wiped the tears from my face with the palms of her hands. She smiled shakily. "No one could ever have been more my real child than you. But you still have to go to school."

I nodded. "I'll go."

"The no-eyebrows bit doesn't make it any easier, does it?" Her hands were still on my cheeks, and she was looking at me with so much understanding that I wanted to bawl again.

Dad crooked a finger at me and began walking backward. "Follow me. I want to try something."

In his studio we stood under one of the skylights that he'd put in himself, the one that leaks every time it rains. He tilted my chin while he painted acrylic eyebrows on me with fine, hairlike strokes.

"Would you like a little heart in each cheekbone,

85

too? No? OK. Let's see what you think."

I went in the bathroom and he followed, wiping his brush on a rag. In the mirror I saw the painted look was definitely better. Better than I deserved, since I'd done this stupid thing to myself.

I smiled at Dad, who lounged against the bathroom door. "Thanks."

He nodded and said, "*Prego*," which is Italian for "You're welcome."

I hugged him.

"I'll go get ready for school," I said.

Clemmie and I met as usual at the bottom of her path. I could tell she was stunned by my new look. She stared hard and said, "You're serious!" several times in a row. But when I explained how and why I'd taken my regular eyebrows off, she was quite admiring.

"That was clever, Susan," she said.

"It didn't change a thing, though," I said, "except the way I look." I bent to pet Douglas Dog, who had come as usual to escort us to the corner.

We walked slowly while I told her about Mr. and Mrs. Stobbel, Harry and Barbara. About the way they looked, the finger cracking, Mr. Stobbel's soft, bearded voice. I told about the cappuccino. I told her about the weekend coming up and the whole month of July and that awful word . . . after.

A hummingbird drank from the Rodriguezes' red-apple feeder, then streaked away. I told her about Grandma and Grandpa Moretti. "She's my best hope. But she's so far away. Thousands and thousands of miles. Just bugging Dad may not do it. And Grandpa Lucas! He's up north with the mooses."

"So you're really going to the Stobbels'!" Clemmie's voice was the voice of doom.

"Initially," I said. "But who knows? I'm working at being the most obnoxious kid they ever saw. It's hard because, you know, I don't want the Stobbels to think Mom and Dad didn't teach me manners, but if I'm nasty enough, I'm hoping they'll decide they don't want me."

"Talk with your mouth full," Clemmie advised. "Grown-ups hate that. And if you have a cold, don't wipe your nose. Let it get all gooby."

"Ugh," I said. "I don't think I could. I'm never going to wash my hair. And I'll have the grossest nails you ever saw. I'll stick them in the dirt. They must have dirt in Laguna Niguel."

"And sulk." Clemmie was really getting into this. "Sophia sulks when she doesn't get her own way, and it drives Mom crazy. Sophia stays in her room, or she doesn't talk for days and days. I love it."

"I have another idea," I told her. "You know how your parents get upset when you're mean to your little brothers? Well, I have a little brother now, and I'm going to be so rotten to him . . ."

"Great," Clemmie said. "He'll whine and tattle . . ."

"And they'll be on *his* side because he's little and they've had him forever and I'm . . . I mean . . ." I swallowed. "I'm a stranger."

"It'll be easy to be rotten to him," Clemmie said. "Little brothers are such dweebs."

I was thinking of the way Jeremy had wrapped the alligator in star paper and sent it to me, and I wasn't sure how easy it would be. I'd do it anyway. "Oh, and I almost forgot to tell you," I said. "When I'm eighteen I'm going to be super rich."

"You're serious!" Clemmie looked at me with respect. "How neat!"

"I'd rather be poor forever and stay here," I said.

We scuffed along in silence after that, not even bothering to be careful of sidewalk cracks. Stepping on them can break your mother's back. But which mother? We didn't even bother to roll our eyes and faint when Andy Luckinbill zoomed past us on his bike. It was hard to believe he was first in line to be my future husband.

Once Clemmie thought of something and got excited for a minute. "Do you know Marcie Trumbull? She goes to our church and she's all the time pulling her knuckles during the sermon. You don't think she could be related to Mrs. Stobbel instead of you?"

"That's a little far out," I said.

"Well, when you're rich, let's go to Rio," Clemmie said at last. "By that time I'll be slim and gorgeous as Sophia, and your eyebrows will have grown back and we'll both have great . . ." She made a rounded motion over her top and pointed to mine. "We'll be great there, and those Rio beaches are fabulous. I've seen them on television. It'll be something to look forward to."

"OK."

We locked thumbs in a solemn promise and I felt a little better. Not much, but a little.

"Have you told me everything now?" Clemmie asked. "You haven't forgotten something else, the way you forgot the money?"

I shook my head no. But of course there were two things I hadn't told her and couldn't. The way Mom and Mrs. Stobbel had clung together, the sudden oneness of them. And the way I'd told Mom she wasn't my mother anymore.

Clemmie and I were still standing, facing each other.

"There's something else I could do to the Stobbels," I said. "Something I could say. The worst ever. I know how I could hurt them a lot."

"How? What?" Clemmie clutched at her heart.

"I could say: 'Why do you want me? You didn't take such good care of the daughter you had. Marlene's *dead*.'"

"Oh Susan! You couldn't!"

"I could," I said. "I definitely could."

Chapter 10

We arrived at John Wayne Airport at ten thirty on Saturday morning.

"See?" Dad tapped his watch. "It took less than an hour from San José, Susie Q. It's just like getting on a bus. We're here," he told Mom gently, and pried her fingers off the arm of her seat.

The Stobbels and Jeremy were there to meet us. He stood so small and scared-looking between his tall, stork father and his rolypoly mom. He wore red shorts and a red-and-white-striped T-shirt and those little kid sandals that have cut-out designs on the straps. His hair was dark and curly, and around his forehead was a paper band with feathers stuck in it. I couldn't stop watching him as we came closer, and though he'd pulled back so he was half hidden by his mom, I could see he was watching me, too.

"Little monster," I told myself. "Just wait and see how rotten I will be to you."

The two adults stepped forward to hug me. I stood stiff and unsmiling. I'm here in body, I told them silently, that's all. Mom took my hand, I guess to comfort me, but I let mine slide away. There was this awful feeling inside me. I didn't want to belong to the Stobbels, but I wasn't Mom and Dad's anymore either. I was nobody.

We stopped in a clump, just inside the sliding glass doors. "How was the flight? Do you have to wait for luggage? No? Well, I can carry something. Susan, give me your duffel." That was Mr. Stobbel, smiling down at me through his beard, comfortable-looking in loose khaki pants and a cobalt-blue T-shirt. Mrs. Stobbel was dressed exactly the same. When they turned, I saw they had "Harry's Pool Service" and a phone number printed across their backs. I decided that advertising on your own body was really tacky and if they were your true parents you'd be totally embarrassed.

"The wagon's just outside." There was the unmistakable crack as Mrs. Stobbel pulled on her fingers.

The wagon was white, with "Harry's Pool Service" and the phone number on the driver's door. A stencil of a cobalt-blue pool and three palm trees adorned the side.

The three of them sat in front and the three of us in back as we drove out of the parking lot, past an enormous bronze statue of John Wayne on an enormous bronze horse. I was beginning to have a dreamy feeling. It was all too weird, like Dorothy in the Land of Oz. Soon I'd wake up and I'd be home in bed in my own room with the sun shivering through the leaves of the lemon tree outside.

Directly ahead of me was the top of Jeremy's curly head with the red and yellow feathers fanning up in front.

Mrs. Stobbel half turned. "We're so glad you're finally here, Susan. We've all been impatient. Particularly Jeremy."

The feathers disappeared as he slunk lower in the seat.

We drove along a wide boulevard lined with tall glass buildings, then onto a freeway. Dad asked Mr. Stobbel polite questions about population and area growth, which I knew he wasn't interested in at all.

Now Jeremy had turned and was kneeling with his chin resting on the back of his seat watching me. One finger came up and slowly traced the curve of his right eyebrow, then the curve of the other, while he stared at my painted ones.

"Hi," Dad said, and immediately he disappeared again.

Mom gazed out her window. Once Dad asked: "Are you OK, honey?" He leaned across me to touch her knee, and she turned and nodded, her eyes invisible behind her dark glasses.

Jeremy had popped up again. He studied me with his head on one side. "Are you 'lergic?" he asked at last.

"Am I what?"

"He means 'allergic.'" Mrs. Stobbel rubbed his red-and-white-striped back. "Marlene was allergic to just about everything, poor little girl."

Jeremy pointed a finger at me. "Are you?"

"No," I said.

Mom kept on staring out of the window. "I am. I'm allergic to just about everything, too."

Everyone sat very still except Jeremy, who began licking the back of his seat till his mom saw him and told him to stop.

"It's good that you're *not*, Susan, 'cause you know why? 'Cause now I can get a kitty. I've never had a kitty. Have you?"

I didn't answer, so Dad answered for me. "Susan hasn't either."

Jeremy bounced up and down, his feathers wafting a breeze in our direction.

"We're going to get the kitty soon but we couldn't till we found out if Susan's 'lergic because she's going to be living in our house."

Mom's head gave a nervous little jerk.

"She's going to be living in our house *some* of the time, Jeremy," Mr. Stobbel corrected. "Remember?"

"You said a lot of the time," Jeremy argued. "A lot is more than some, isn't it Mom?"

Mrs. Stobbel laughed an embarrassed laugh. "There's no fooling you, is there, sweetheart?"

"Well, here's our turn-off," Mr. Stobbel said. I thought he was probably pretty glad to see it.

"When we moved here, just after Marlene was born . . ." He paused. "Just after Marlene and Susan were born, I guess . . . there were hardly any homes. Now look at them."

It was hard not to look at them. The green hillside was ribboned with houses. They wound up and over and along the crests. Everywhere signs announced OCEAN VIEW. SMALL DOWN PAYMENT. 100% FINANCING.

"Where's the ocean?" Dad asked.

"On the other side of the highway. You actually can see it if you are high enough."

We drove for miles with houses snaking around us, passing bulldozers that butted the land to make room for more.

I saw the disbelieving look on Dad's face and broke my sulky silence. "It's not much like Santa Cruz, is it?" I whispered.

"It *is* a bit overwhelming at first," Mr. Stobbel said. "But this is Southern California, and the people who come here have to live somewhere. When Barbara and I feel like complaining, we stop ourselves fast. After all, we came. What gives us the right to shut the door on everybody else? And it really is nice down here."

"Susan," Jeremy asked in his little demanding voice, "will you come swimming with me?"

"I don't like to swim."

Mom sighed and said in a tired voice, "Of course you do. You swim in the university pool every chance you get."

Jeremy had his hands clasped in front of him. "Please, Susan. Please."

Already I could tell Jeremy was going to be the hardest Stobbel to resist. But I would.

Mr. Stobbel was driving through gates set in a low brick wall. PARADISE BLUFFS, PRIVATE, the notice said.

Jeremy rubbed his cheek shyly against his mom's shoulder. "Did you like the present I sent you, Susan? My alligator?"

Don't look at him, I told myself. Be tough. "Not really," I said. "It's a baby toy."

His smile disappeared and I saw his mom rub his back again.

Dad said: "Susan! Honey!" and suddenly I felt like

crying. Who would have thought being mean would be this hard?

Now we were pulling into the driveway of a blue-and-gray two-story house. It had a little window, like a porthole, high in the eaves. Jeremy pointed, "That's my room, way up there." He watched me warily now and his voice was unsure.

Mr. Stobbel stopped the wagon beside a truck with a load of stuff in its open back and the words "Harry's Pool Service" on the door.

We all got out.

"Look, there's our whale!" Jeremy pointed to a weathervane on the pointed roof, where a metal whale stood motionless on its stand. He dashed to the front door. "And this is our house."

I was glad he knew. You could get lost in this swamp of houses all with their high porthole windows and tidy gardens. Only the paint colors seemed different.

The Stobbels had a wreath of dried flowers on the door and a perching fake robin. The doormat said, "The Stobbels." I hated it all. I had such a longing for home, for Mrs. Cram's crazy used-furniture yard, for my own higgledy-piggledy street with its mixture of big and little houses. For fleabag Douglas Dog. For Clemmie.

The street was a dead end and there were lots of little kids on tricycles and scooters. They came wheeling over, circling us like Indians circling a covered wagon.

Somebody called: "Is that your new sister, Jeremy?"

Jeremy nodded. "Her name's Susan."

Mom gasped. "They all know? They know about the mistake . . . and Susan and Marlene?"

Mr. Stobbel stroked his beard. "No. The kids know Jeremy's getting a new sister. It's hard to keep an excited four-year-old quiet. But they think we're adopting. Some of our friends, the ones we can trust, know the whole story. It *is* bound to get out, I'm afraid, sooner or later, but we'll hold it as long as we can."

A girl of about eight had edged in close to us. She fiddled with an end of her long blond hair. "She sure isn't as pretty as Marlene was."

"Oh, Brittany!" Mrs. Stobbel gave a loud, exasperated sigh. "That's not very nice."

Brittany tossed her head. "It's true. She has a weird face. What happened to her eyebrows?"

And then I felt Jeremy's hot little hand pushing into mine. "You leave her alone, bratty Brittany. She's my sister and she's nicer than you." His voice was high and shrill, like an angry bird's, and he was pulling me quickly up the path toward the door. "Come on.

98

Don't listen to her. You are too pretty. And your face isn't super weird."

I couldn't believe he was defending me when I'd been such a yuk to him.

"We've got a big surprise for you," he whispered, then put his hand over his mouth. "I'm not supposed to tell."

Mr. Stobbel opened the door. Stretched across the inside hallway was a paper banner decorated with cutout flowers. Printed in squiggly letters were the words WELCOME, SUSAN.

Jeremy hopped up and down. "I made it. I made it. I wanted to put WELCOME HOME, SUSAN, but Mom and Dad said I shouldn't because that might mix you up." His feathers had slipped down over one eye and Mrs. Stobbel straightened them. I noticed how smooth and tanned and pretty her arms were. She half laughed. "Never tell anything to Jeremy that you don't want repeated. He doesn't know the meaning of the word 'tact.'"

"I do too. It's . . . it's . . ." Jeremy gave up.

Mom and Dad and I stood in the hallway beneath the banner. To the right was the living room with pale-blue carpeting and a deeper-blue couch. To the left was the dining room, the table set with six blue place mats. There was a bowl of flowers in the center. I thought they must be fake like the robin because they looked like blue roses, and I thought how much I detested phony flowers, but then I remembered how Marlene was 'lergic. Probably they couldn't have real flowers in the house. We couldn't either, but at least we didn't pretend with artificial ones.

I stood there, looking around, and my heart was hammering. If the hospital hadn't made a mistake twelve years ago, this was where I'd have lived for all of my life. I'd have sat at that table for meals, maybe for Thanksgiving with relatives I didn't even know yet. I might have curled up on that couch, snuggled into the striped pillows, reading or looking out the window at the kids playing in the street. I glanced at Mom and Dad. They stood very still, holding hands, and I knew instantly that their thoughts were like mine, but different. They were realizing that their daughter, their Marlene, had lived here. She'd eaten at that table, sat on that couch. Dad put his arm around Mom and pulled her close.

"Can we go outside now and show them the pool and the 'cuzi?" Jeremy had found a battered-looking teddy bear, maybe on the stairs, and he was throwing it in the air, letting it fall, tossing it again.

"I think maybe they'd like to go up and see their rooms first," Mr. Stobbel said. "Come on, Jeremy. You take Susan's bag." He gave Jeremy the duffel, and it almost made me laugh the way his little legs buckled under the weight. Except that I definitely was not going to laugh for any reason this weekend, or smile either.

Mom and Dad and I followed them, Mrs. Stobbel bringing up the rear. "I hope you'll be comfortable," she said. "We have . . ." Mom and Dad had stopped at the top of the staircase. The door to the right was closed. I don't know how they knew. Maybe parents have some kind of special sense. Mrs. Stobbel was still a few steps below us, and she stopped, too. "That was Marlene's room," she said.

We stared at the closed door.

I swallowed. Oh no. Please no. Please don't say this is where I'm to sleep tonight.

"We gave almost everything of hers to the thrift shop that's run by Children's Hospital." Mr. Stobbel's voice was as soft as his wife's. "But we kept some things that we couldn't bear to part with. We put them away."

Dad nodded, and Mom fumbled with the rims of her dark glasses, which she'd kept on, even though we were inside the house.

"Would you like to see the room?" Mrs. Stobbel wasn't asking me, she was asking Mom and Dad.

"Yes," Mom whispered. "Please."

Mr. Stobbel stepped past us. There were four small holes in the door and I knew instantly that there'd been one of those little nameplates there. It had probably been white with flowers around it and it had said MARLENE'S ROOM, the way my playhouse at home said SUSAN'S ROOM. I imagined Mr. Stobbel taking it off after Marlene died, taking out the screws that had fixed it to the door. It would have been hard for him, like saying good-bye to Marlene all over again. But he wouldn't want his wife to have to keep seeing it every time she came up the stairs. MARLENE'S ROOM. And Marlene gone forever. Maybe the little nameplate was one of the things they'd saved, that they couldn't bear to give up. He opened the door.

The room was empty of everything. There were four small indentations on the yellow rug where the feet of a bed had been and four more where a dresser might have stood. The wallpaper was white with a green fern pattern. Through the window I could see the railings of a small white balcony.

I glanced at Jeremy. He'd gone very quiet and he held the teddy bear up so it half covered his face, and peered around it. The one eye I could see brimmed over with tears.

"We're going to have this for a little upstairs den," Mrs. Stobbel said. "We'll get one of those small TVs, bookcases." Her voice faltered. "Sometime soon, we'll do it. When we can handle it." She glanced at me.

"Susan, we have a guest room and well . . . when

you come, we thought it would be nice to decorate it specially for you. Your favorite colors."

And a nameplate SUSAN'S ROOM, I thought. Oh, but thank goodness they weren't going to make me have this one.

"This is a prettier room," Mrs. Stobbel said. "But I didn't think you'd want it to be yours."

"No." I almost added, "I don't want any room here to be mine," but she looked so sad and I was sad myself. Too sad to be horrible. And wasn't it strange how she'd known the way I'd feel about this? But maybe it wasn't so strange. Not if she was really my mother.

Mom and Dad stood a little to one side, in front of me. They had their arms around each other. And suddenly I had that horrible, left-out, abandoned and forgotten feeling again. The nobody feeling.

Then Dad looked over his shoulder and said: "Susan? Susan, come here, sweetheart," and when I went he put his other arm around me so the three of us were together again. I knew it was his way of telling me that I was still part of them. But I knew I wasn't. Not really. Not anymore.

Chapter 11

"You're sleeping in my room tonight," Jeremy told me when we were outside again in the upper hallway, Marlene's door safely closed behind us. "I'm going to be with Mom and Dad in my new Batman sleeping bag." He huffed and puffed as he dragged my duffel behind him. "Your other mom and dad will be in the guest room, 'cause they're guests. You're not. You're my sister."

I let that go. There was no point in arguing with a four-year-old. He opened a door and I saw his room, all reds and blues with airplanes that dangled from the ceiling and one of those maple beds that has drawers underneath. He lugged my duffel into the middle of the room.

"I'm supposed to bring you down for lunch now,"

he told me importantly. "I know what we're having."

What we had was chicken salad nicely mounded on dark-green lettuce leaves.

I remembered to chew with my mouth open. *Chomp, chomp, chomp.* Too bad I didn't know how to burp. Clemmie knows and she's tried to teach me, but I can't get it. *Chomp, chomp, chomp.*

Jeremy watched me with interest, then went *chomp, chomp, chomp* too. I could see all the disgusting chewed-up chicken inside his mouth.

"Excuse us for a minute, Barbara," Dad said. His face was tight. He stood and motioned for me to come with him.

In the hallway he gripped my shoulders. "Susan, just stop this nonsense, now. I can see you have a plan cooked up to be as revolting as you know how. Well, Barbara and Harry are just going to figure they'll have to work hard on your table manners. In the meantime none of us can enjoy our lunch. Stop it! Understand?"

I nodded. Grandma might call Dad a wimp, but he isn't really. And when he uses that voice, I know I'd better listen. Anyway, chewing like that is hard work. My ears and jaws ached.

"It's just, I don't know if I'm going to be able to handle being here," I said. "They're so not like us."

"Oh Susan!" Dad closed his eyes and shook his head. "Think what you're saying. They're not like us and we're better. Our taste is good, theirs stinks. Do you have any idea how much pain in the world starts with that kind of thing?"

I spread my hands. "What did I say? I didn't say any of that."

"You know that's what you were thinking. So just quit it, OK?"

I nodded. And I didn't try anything for the rest of the meal.

As soon as we'd finished, Jeremy asked: "Can Susan and I go swimming?"

"I didn't bring a suit," I said.

"Can you come and watch me then? Please?"

"Maybe we should all sit outside," Mr. Stobbel suggested. "You go change, Jeremy."

As soon as we stepped through the glass doors into the garden, Mom caught her breath. "Oh, this is lovely, really lovely."

Her voice was warm, but I saw the way she held her dark blazer closed, with her arms tight around herself. I saw her shiver.

The garden was small, with bright green grass and some kind of crawling shrub that half hid the metal fence at the back. Beyond was nothing but space. The house sat on the curve of an open valley, furzy and wild, with other houses winding around the valley's rim. Way, way in the distance were mountains, shadowed by purple haze.

Dad shaded his eyes. "What a view."

"That's the advantage of being one of the first families here. They don't all have it this nice. Just six homes, actually." Mr. Stobbel unlatched the gate that led from the garden into a fenced area, and I saw a round pool attached to a round Jacuzzi so they made a figure eight. Water flowed over the smaller top circle into the lower one to make a shallow waterfall.

A small tornado launched itself through the gate. "Here I come," Jeremy yelled, streaking past us in a flash of yellow swim trunks and skinny brown body.

"Susan, Susan, are you watching?" he shrieked, flinging himself into the pool, showering us in a rainbow sparkle of water.

He was doing some kind of dog paddle, coming up to breathe, paddling ferociously again. He scrambled out, belly-flopped back in.

"Slow *down*," his mother called.

"He's going to be showing off every second he's in there," Mr. Stobbel said fondly. "Little water rat. How about if the rest of you go sit in comfort?" He waved toward white metal chairs on the grassy lawn. "I'll stay in here and keep an eye on him."

"No, I will," I said quickly. It would be better than

being with *them*, watching Mom, wondering if she was all right, watching Dad watching Mom, all of them doing their best to make friendly conversation, Mrs. Stobbel's knuckles cracking.

"You don't mind?" Mr. Stobbel asked.

I shook my head and bent to unbuckle my sandals.

It was nice sitting in the sun between the two pools, my feet dangling in the splash of the waterfall. Beyond the fence a small, rough path wound around, and I saw two women joggers on it. On the slope a boy about my age played Frisbee with a small black dog. I thought of our backyard at home. The chairs that we've had forever with their faded canvas seats, the wooden table that we could never eat at because it was covered with broken pots and trowels and flats of herbs waiting to be planted. I told myself that I liked our yard better and that I didn't really like this at all, because to like it, to like anything here, would be wrong. I shouldn't and I wouldn't.

Every now and then Jeremy would pull on my foot to make sure I was watching him. "See this? See what I can do?"

Once he said, in a small voice: "If you don't like my al'gator, would you bring him back when you come?"

"*If* I come back," I said.

He blinked up at me, eyes red from the chlorine.

108

"You mean you might not?"

I shrugged. "I don't know."

"When Marlene went away that day, she never came back," he said sadly. So weird to think of things like that. If she had come back, if she hadn't been killed, no one would have known about the mistake. There'd have been no tests, nothing. Everybody would have stayed happy.

Jeremy was clinging to the side of the pool. "Do you have any grandparents?" I asked. "Or aunts or uncles?"

"Hundreds." He sounded unsure. "Is that good? Do you like grandmas and grandpas and aunts and uncles?"

I nodded. I liked my own. I wasn't sure about his.

"There's Grandma and Grandpa Morgan and Grandma and Grandpa Stobbel and Aunt Donna and Uncle Richard and Aunt Jenny and . . ." He screwed up his face, considering. "Oh yes, there's Uncle Zack and Cousin Joey and . . ."

"Great," I muttered. "Hundreds is right."

He hung out from the side watching me. "They like you. They wanted to come over today and meet you, even Aunt Donna and she lives real far away. But Mom said they couldn't. She said it would be too much. She said it would be too hard for you. She said

109

there'd be lots of time after."

After, I thought. That has to be the world's scariest word.

When a voice spoke close to my left shoulder, I almost lost my balance. "Hi, Jeremy!"

I spun around. It was the Frisbee boy, the dog halfway up the slope panting behind him.

"Hi, Tony," Jeremy called. "Watch this. I can dive now." He scrabbled up the side and flung himself back in. "Did you see me, Tony? Did you?"

Tony threw the Frisbee and the dog bounded off. "I saw you, Jeremy."

Jeremy pointed. "That's Susan, my new sister. She doesn't have a swimsuit and she doesn't have any eyebrows. Those ones are fake."

The boy grinned. "I can see that."

Talk about dweeby little brothers, I thought. Talk about wanting to kill this one.

"Barbara and Harry told us you were coming," he said. I wondered if he knew the whole thing or if he just thought they were adopting me. He nodded toward a house with green trim, two doors down. "I live there. Barbara says you'll be going to our school in the fall. Elwood. It's where Marlene went." He had red hair that flamed in the sunlight and lots and lots of freckles, even on his back and shoulders, which I could see because he wasn't wearing a T-shirt, just cut-off jeans and dirty Nikes.

"I was really sorry about Marlene," he said. "She was nice."

"Susan *might* be nice," Jeremy said, considering. "We're not sure yet. Mom and Dad says it may take some time."

"Oh man!" I rolled my eyes.

Tony grinned again, and I noticed that he had real cute gaps between his top teeth. They were the kind of gaps you could stick straws through and cause a sensation in the cafeteria. I began to wish I had bangs, or a sun visor that I could pull mysteriously down over my eyes. I was wishing like heck that I had eyebrows.

By now the adults had spotted him and Mr. Stobbel was calling "Hi" and asking "How are things going, Tony?" and telling Mom and Dad how this was Tony Lewis and how he'd crewed on their sailboat in the last Catalina race.

By then the little black dog was back with the Frisbee.

"I'd better go," Tony said. "Basil's getting impatient."

"'Bye. 'Bye, Basil."

I turned to watch the two of them stroll along the path. It mustn't be true that people with red hair and

111

freckles didn't tan, because his hair was the reddest I'd ever seen and . . .

"Susan, Susan . . ." Little voice, gurgling and spluttering.

I stood quickly, almost falling in. Where was Jeremy?

And then I saw him, underwater, coming up, his head breaking the surface, arms flailing, sinking again, so that standing up I could see him, hanging there suspended like a fish in the water.

Oh no! Had he jumped and hit his head? What?

"Barbara!" I screamed. "Harry!" I just had time to see them swing around, to see them start up, a chair overturning, to hear somebody shout "Jeremy!" before I leaped into the pool, splashing, struggling to get to him.

He popped up. I grabbed his hair and heard him yelp: "Hey! Stop that! Quit, you're hurting." I loosened my hold, and he was giggling. "Fooled you! Fooled you!"

And now I saw the adult feet and legs by the side of the pool. I had my arms hooked under Jeremy's arms, holding him up, and he was pushing me away. "Let go, Susan. You're squeezing me too tight. It was just a trick."

Mr. Stobbel's voice was grim and his face was grim, too. "Jeremy! Out! Now!" He didn't wait for Jeremy to obey, bending over, scooping him up to stand dripping on the cement.

"We've told you and told you that's not funny," he said. I clung to the pool shivering and shaking with fear.

"I just wanted to show Susan my drowning trick," Jeremy whimpered.

"Poor Susan! Look! You scared her half to death. Here, honey . . ." Mr. Stobbel leaned over and held out his hands. "Come on, I'll help you get out. Barbara, find some towels, will you?"

Mom and Dad crowded around me. "We didn't see him . . ." Mom began.

"He knew we weren't paying attention," Mr. Stobbel said angrily. "That's why he did it. I'm sure mad at you, Jeremy. There's enough real danger in the world without pretending. No more swimming for you all day, young man. And none tomorrow either." He turned to me. "Susan, are you all right?"

I'd never been so cold in all my life. My teeth were chattering. My legs trembled. I clutched at Mr. Stobbel's sleeve. "I guess . . . I think . . ."

Jeremy bit his lip. "I'm sorry, Susan. I just wanted you to see how good I do it."

I looked at the littleness of him, the skinniness, the big pleading eyes, and I was remembering the flood of terror, when I wondered if I'd get to him in time.

I remembered the need to save him that was maybe stronger than anything I'd ever felt in my life. And I knew.

"It's OK," I whispered. "I'm just glad . . ." The words were stuck somewhere. I kneeled down and hugged him, hard.

"Ow, you're all drippy and your clothes are cold." He tried to pull away. "And yuk, you should see! You look horrible! One of your eyebrows washed off."

I laughed and squeezed him even tighter. "You little dweeb," I whispered. "You little monster. I hate you."

"If that doesn't sound just like a sister," Mrs. Stobbel said.

Chapter 12

Clemmie called that night.

"Can you talk?" she asked.

"Sure," I said. "I'm the only one here. We've just had dinner by the pool and they're still outside. I'm sitting at the dining-room table." I almost added, "next to the blue fake roses," but I didn't. It seemed like a put-down, and I wasn't sure I wanted to put Harry and Barbara down anymore. And when had I started thinking of them as Harry and Barbara, anyway?

"Oh la-di-da," Clemmie said. "Dinner by the pool. It doesn't sound too bad. Tell me everything. Is the plan working? Are they hating you? Have you said the awful thing yet?"

I ran my fingers lightly over the phone buttons.

"Well, no. I haven't had a chance."

"Oh." I could hear Clemmie thinking, coming to conclusions.

"You *like* them," she said at last in a flat, disappointed voice. "You've decided to stay there and not come back."

"No," I said. "I'll never decide that." I turned so I could see outside, could see the four of them sitting around the glass table, the dark mountains and the shine of the night sky behind them. My four. How strange! "I'll always go back . . . come back. Clemmie, I don't know anymore which is go and which is come. There are two places now. Call me tomorrow when I get home, OK? You can help me figure it out."

There was a long pause, and then Clemmie asked: "What's the little turkey of a brother like?"

"He's not bad," I said casually.

"Are there other kids our age around?"

"I met one. His name's Tony Lewis. We'll be going to the same school."

"Cute?" Clemmie asked.

"Great teeth," I said, and then held the phone away as she shrieked: "Tony Lewis. You're serious! You mean Anthony Lewis?"

"I guess. What is it? Do you know him or something?"

"No, gooney! But I'm talking A.L. Andy Luckinbill

116

and Anthony Lewis. You have a possible husband in both places."

I sighed. "Don't be so lame, Clemmie." But I felt a little shiver of excitement. A.L. That *was* pretty weird.

"Well, anyway," Clemmie said, "I'm dieting my brains out to be ready for Rio. I don't think it's going to work, though. I've decided I'm destined to be capital F-A-T fat."

Outside I saw Barbara getting up, coming toward the house. She was wearing a silky peach-colored dress with a straight skirt and I thought she looked super nice.

"Capital F-A-T fat isn't all that bad," I told Clemmie, "if you have other things going for you. I have to hang up now," and I did, right in the middle of her astonished silence. I was pretty astonished myself.

Barbara slid the glass door back and came inside.

"Hi," she said. "Guess what *I'm* going to make."

I shook my head. "I don't know."

"Cappuccino. From a package I bought. Want to help?" She pressed her hands together and a knuckle went snap. Immediately she put her hands in her pockets. "I'm sorry. I know that drives everyone crazy. It drives me crazy. It's just . . . you know . . . when I'm scared."

"Scared? Really?"

"Of course, scared silly. Scared of you." She gave me a shaky smile, then walked past me to the cabinet and took out a package. "Let's see. This can't be all that hard. First we boil the water."

"Shall I put on the kettle?" It was hard for me to speak normally.

"Yes, please."

She put five cups and saucers and a glass of apple juice on a blue tray. "The juice is for Jeremy," she said.

"I think I'd prefer juice, too," I told her, and she smiled, touched my cheek with the tip of her finger, and poured another glass. It was the only time she'd touched me, except for that first day when she took my hand that I'd made limp as a wet sock, and this morning, that awful, stiff hug at the airport. It was the first time we'd been alone together. I wished I knew how to crack my knuckles if that really helped a person be less scared. But it was probably like burping . . . hard to learn.

We stood side by side, waiting for the water to boil.

"Susan?"

My heart hammered. I knew something was coming, something serious.

"I know you think Harry and I shouldn't be asking to share your life."

It was true. And now was the time to make my rotten accusation. But I couldn't force the words out. I moved the handles of the cups so they were all turned neatly in the same direction.

"But once we knew about you, there was this . . . this pull," she said.

I mumbled something. Awful to admit, but I was feeling a small pull myself.

It was tough getting Jeremy to go to bed even though Barbara and Harry let him stay up an extra half hour.

"I'll read you a story," I said.

He held up two fingers.

"One," I said firmly.

When I'd helped him wriggle into his Batman bag, I sat cross-legged on the floor beside him and read *Frog and Toad Together*, which he said was his favorite book. Sometimes he said the words with me: *"Frog, I am glad to have a brave friend like you," said Toad.*

Jeremy sat up. "You were brave, Susan."

"No, I wasn't. Lie down. *Toad was asleep and he was having a dream.*"

"I'm not asleep," Jeremy said.

But I knew he was getting close. He was tugging at his hair, and his eyes were half closed. I tug my hair when I'm getting sleepy. I've always done that, ever since I was little.

Barbara's faint, flowery scent drifted around the room. I turned the page very quietly and made my voice very quiet, too. *"'Frog, Frog, where have you gone?' Toad was spinning in the dark. 'Come back, Frog,' he shouted. 'I will be lonely!' 'I am right here,' said Frog."*

"Susan?" Jeremy said. "I will be lonely if you don't come back. I was awful lonely when Marlene left." His hand slipped out, and I held it and sat very still. My legs were aching. Clemmie's sister, Sophia, could sit like that for hours. She said she was meditating, but Clemmie said she was just thinking about Boomer Thompson and about getting married.

"Susan? Will you promise never to call me 'Germy'? Some kids do when they're being mean."

I smiled. "Germy, huh? I like that."

I thought he was asleep until he said again, "Susan?"

"Yes?"

"Susan? Do you think Marlene will mind if I love you, too?"

"No," I said. "It doesn't mean you have to stop loving her. It doesn't work that way."

"Good."

I heard his breathing get louder. His hand slipped from mine. He was asleep at last.

Later, when I was in bed myself, my door opened silently. And there was Mom in her soft flowered nightgown. I made room so she could sit next to me, and I took her hand the way Jeremy had taken mine. Outside, a coyote called from somewhere deep in the wild, dry valley.

I was the first to speak. "Is this going to work out, Mom?"

"I don't know, Susan. Dad and I keep telling ourselves it could be worse. But I keep thinking it could be better, too. It could never have happened."

"If only Marlene hadn't died," I said, and then I added, "I'm sorry, Mom. Sorry, sorry."

"That's OK. I know you didn't mean it that way. It's . . ."

I interrupted. "I really am sorry about her."

Mom's head drooped. "Tomorrow, on the way to the airport, we're going to stop at her grave. You won't mind, Susan?"

"No." Mom has a little scar in the soft place between her thumb and finger. I've known the feel of that scar all my life. I smoothed it gently.

"Maybe we should have run off with you, fought for you right at the beginning. Maybe we still should."

I wove my fingers through hers. "You couldn't. I think I understand that now. I didn't before."

"What is it you understand, love?"

"About the pull. It was there for you, too, wasn't it? The pull back to Marlene."

Mom brought our hands up, the fingers still joined,

and rubbed them against her cheek. "Oh sweetie, you've had to grow up so fast. You don't sound like my little girl anymore."

"Oh, but I am," I said.

Jeremy's hanging planes made moonlit wing shadows on the bed.

"I know I have to come back here. I know it's legal and I have to, and I'm not dreading it as much as I thought I would. But I'm going to be home a lot. Like half and half. I am! I'll beg and I'll plead, and if that doesn't work I'll howl and . . ." I stopped for breath. "They'll have to let me."

"I don't think you'll need to do anything that drastic. I think they'll let you."

"And I want to say something else, Mom. Maybe I'll get to care for Barbara and Harry a bit, you know, after a while. But if I do, it won't mean I'll ever stop loving you and Dad."

Mom stroked my hair. "Is this the 'love isn't a candy bar' theory? You understand now that the more you give, the more you have left to give?" There were tears in her voice.

"Sort of," I said. "Mom? Will you always keep my room just the way it is? My playhouse, the lantern, everything?"

She leaned over and kissed me. "Everything, Susan," she said. "Everything. Always."